The Battle of Dungalo

Stephen Newman

Praise for the Book

This was such a fun, quirky read! I've read quite a number of folktales, but nothing quite like this.

The Battle of Dungalo incorporates modern concepts in a classic genre and I never thought that combination was something I'd see, but I thoroughly enjoyed it.

I especially loved how fleshed out most characters are. Although it's quite humorous at some parts, you can see the deeper, intriguing psyche of the characters. Quite refreshing in a genre that doesn't go too deep into that.

- Agatha Inwang

*　　*　　*

An interesting and imaginative novel. Stephen Newman, whom I have known as a family friend for more than twenty years, has poured his creativity and heart into this story. *The Battle of*

Dungalo is not only engaging but also rich with meaning, weaving together themes of courage, unity, and hope. It is a book that both entertains and inspires, and I wholeheartedly recommend it to readers of all ages."

- *Mrs. Charlotte Botchway*

*   *   *

This is a fascinating novel that is both imaginative and inspiring.

- *Mrs. Agnes Addo-Danso*

Table of Contents

Acknowledgment

I would like to express my heartfelt gratitude to my wife, Cathrine Newman, for her support and encouragement throughout the writing of this book. A special thank you goes to my children–Michelle, Alexandra, and Mark–for their love, patience and inspiration along the way.

My deepest appreciation also goes to my editor, Agatha Inwang, and to my publisher, Joy Ani, along with the dedicated team at *Joy of Many Generations*. Your guidance, meticulous editing, and commitment to bringing this story to life have been instrumental in turning my script into a published work.

To all who played a part in this journey, I remain profoundly grateful.

Chapter One

The great neem tree in The Glebel is just starting to fruit—small, oval balls that are in shades of green and yellow.

There is evidence of it on the ground as well, squashed into the earth by the numerous hoofs and paws that pass by The Glebel frequently, being the central city square where the animals organise their frequent trades and meetings.

A leaf from the neem tree plucks away from its branch and falls gently, briefly landing on the compressed nose of Al, the old orangutan, before falling to the ground by his clawed feet.

Al sniffs and impatiently rubs an orange-furred hand across his nose before looking on to the central stage that had been set up to accommodate the King of Yakko forest, who'd called this very impromptu meeting of all animals.

He had been contemplating not coming, not out of defiance to the new king, but because his bones had grown weary and tired, along with his mind.

Al has witnessed four reigns of the Yakko Royals, right from when he was a wrinkly youngin clinging to his mother's fur. None of the reigns had particularly inspired a patriotic spirit in him, and if anything was inspired, it was terror that Al had trouble healing his mind from.

No one knows exactly how the reign of the current king will be—ever since he was crowned a year ago, it's been silence on his end, with nothing keeping the animals in check but the memories of the terrors that previously ruled them.

As a young prince, the current king had been a mild character, barely making public appearances, and the animals would have doubted the old king had an heir if not for the occasional glimpses.

Nobody knows the character of the current king, including Al, so he'd rather not risk finding out the hard way when used to make an example for those who chose to skip the gathering.

"God bless the new king; I pray his reign favours us." Nina, the hare, mutters beside Al, triggering a memory from the old reigns.

The one that punished anyone who spoke ill of the king, so much so that the default phrasing before speaking on anything concerning the king was "God bless the king." This way, they were still guaranteed to be home with their family by nightfall.

Al prayed that if this reign of terror still awaited them in this new reign, he'd rather join his ancestors in the great oak tree where their souls resided in peace and without fear.

In the midst of all the quiet chaos, there is a group boldly taking up the space they occupied, with a large ring of empty space around them that no animal dared enter.

This group is called the Royalists, made up of mean-looking vultures that seem to be eternally shrouded in gloom and despair. Which makes sense because they've been the right-hand of the Royals for many, many decades, holding as much power as the command of the King.

Al remembers how coming across a Royalist usually meant that something terrible was about to happen. He would know, because he did once, but that was all it took for him to never see his family again.

However, ever since the new king took the throne, rumours have been circulating that the Royalists and their servants have been let go, and this has significantly impacted their power. For with no royal backing, they can't act too rashly against the animals that can easily wring them out of existence.

And so, they'd been in obscurity since the crowning of the new king, and this is the first time the animals had spotted them back in public.

A chill suddenly descends on the Glebel, and all chatter ceases immediately, in fear of punishment.

The new king — King Migag II — has taken the stage, seen in public for the first time in a year.

King Migag II is still an agile lion, despite having already lived a significant number of years. As he struts to the middle of the enormous stage, there is a quiet confidence in his gait. Despite the terror amongst the animals, there is still appreciation for how magnificent his golden fur and lush mane look, seeming to bounce the hot glare of the sun off and back into the atmosphere.

His wife, the stunning Lioness, Queen Sheila, walks demurely behind him but stops a few steps away from the centre stage, glancing around the large crowd before them in silence. By her side is their son, Prince Edgar, who still has his mane growing in and stands with a meek kind of confidence.

King Migag II looks to the message relayers, long rows of small monkeys hanging by their tails on the branches of trees all the way from the stage to the end of the crowd. They are a trained team responsible for passing along the message to the very back of the crowd that might not have heard the King— even if the voices of the Lions are impossible to ignore.

Their leader at the forefront hoots positively at their readiness and King Migag II subtly nods before looking back at his subjects.

"Animals of Yakko forest, it is my utmost pleasure to be in your midst on this

beautiful day," King Migag II said, his voice a boom that even the best speakers can't replicate. The message relayers on all sides still work hard, making sure the message reaches the end of the crowd barely a second after the King's last word.

Meanwhile, the animals are left in a slight state of confusion at the warmth in the King's greeting. Not one animal in the crowd has ever experienced a King speaking to them without the poisonous lacing of hostility and a condescending tone.

King Migag II continues.

"I am aware that my first official appearance has been long overdue," he says solemnly. "I apologize for the silence in my first official months as your King. It is never wise for a King to make his subjects feel abandoned."

More confusion amongst the animals. Having been used to the hostile ways the former Kings addressed them, King Migag II's respectful tone is starting to feel like an unknown enemy — a threat that brings with it a foreshadowing of greater doom.

It is too unsettling.

"However, I promise you that my silence has not been for naught," King Migag II says, strolling from the middle to the front of the stage. The animals occupying the first five rolls simultaneously take three steps back. He notices and takes one step back.

The Royalists seem to be muttering something amongst themselves, but due to the wide berth given them by every animal around them, no one can catch what they're discussing.

"For the past year, I've been reviewing some seemingly forgotten blueprints for a future that benefits us all." King Migag II says, pacing around the stage, looking to be lost in a distant land filled with thoughts. "I believe every dear animal here would testify to being a direct or indirect witness to the evil that has been continuously inflicted upon us by the savage creatures known as… humans."

There is an involuntary chill that settles upon every animal as King Migag II mentions humans. Some animals gasp in horror; some nearly flee from the square and would've succeeded if not for the crowd; some fall to the ground and start weeping.

Along with the reign of terror of previous kings, one other thing that has taken the peace from countless animals and their generations is the cruel acts of the human race on whichever animal they laid hands on.

Many present would testify to either witnessing their loved ones slain or taken savagely by humans. And if any animal had never witnessed it, they surely heard the stories that promised them nightmares they couldn't recover from.

Humans were the animals' greatest enemies. One reason many feared the Royalists during the reign of the evil kings was because those wicked creatures seemed to work with the savages that inflicted pain upon them.

It was one way they held power over their fellow animals—by promising anyone that refused to do their bidding great suffering that would somehow involve a human. They were never open in their dealings with humans, so many animals never found proof. But it was there — an open secret that no one dared say out loud. Hence, they found a glowing target on their furry, leathery or scaly backs next.

Now in the sunny Glebel, the confident yet warm voice of the king cuts through their terror, like a hug that hasn't been given in lifetimes.

"I come with a solution to end all the misery we've all endured for far too long," King Migag II says, and the animals wait with bated breath. "One that would not only make us the envy of every other kingdom but would also protect us from sadistic foes."

At that moment, two capybaras came up to the stage, rolling a large board draped with a green cloth between them.

The animals look on curiously, and those at the back are starting to regret why they didn't come early enough to find a better spot — but then, the positioning of some animals is intentional, as they don't want to stay too close to a royal, especially not one they can't gauge yet.

The capybaras roll the board to the front of the stage, just beside the king, then dutifully stand on each side, awaiting further instructions.

"Citizens of Yakko Forest and my friends," King Migag II says as he paces back and forth in front of the board. "This is the blueprint for a better future, one I have worked on and reviewed several times with the input of trusted consultants."

There is sudden chattering among the animals as some strain necks to better see what is going on. Some of the smaller creatures scramble up the backs of bigger and taller animals like the giraffes and the elephants to get a premium view.

King Migag II tips his head at the capybaras, and with tiny paws, they simultaneously grab onto the green material.

"I present to you…" King Migag II smiles as the capybaras pull down the material from the board to the surprised gasps of the animals. "The city-state of Dungalo."

Chapter Two

A long time ago, when the reign of the kings of Yakko forest hadn't turned into something so dreadful, the animals thrived in unity — not a perfect one, as they still had the occasional human nuisance bothering them, but at least they were stronger in numbers.

However, there was a clan war between the lions, and half of them were driven far away from Yakko Forest. With them went a number of animals that sided with them in the war.

This was where things started to go downhill. The animals of Yakko forest soon realised that they were stuck on the wrong side of the war with the leader they got, however, it was too late to escape by then.

The King had enlisted the help of the cruel vultures to keep the animals in check, and anyone who tried to escape was terribly punished and, worse, watched their families suffer in the process.

For nearly a century, they had endured each draconian reign. Until King Migag II. At the sunny Glebel, all the animals watched in silence at the blueprint before them.

It highlighted the plans to build a city-state where the animals had humane rights and security they could rely on.

As King Migag II explains the plan for this new city-state, pointing to different sections of the blueprint on the board, the animals can see the excitement and determination in his eyes.

The plans for the city-state of Dungalo do not stop at the reinforced security walls around the kingdom or the plans to establish a trained security force.

There are also plans to create a court of law which ensures that the voices of the animals are heard better and their rights recognised. This is the biggest shock of all in the blueprint King Migag II presents.

No selfish king would ever give his subjects the option to be able to challenge his say. The kings of old held on strongly to their voices being the only true power, never to be challenged.

What King Migag II is doing is incredibly selfless, not to mention humble, knowing that he has plans to give the animals the power to resist his say.

There is one thing obvious in all of this:

The King really is determined to create this city of Dungalo as a safe haven for his citizens.

"Now, I do not expect this to go without the occasional bumps or flaws," King Migag II says as he starts to round off his presentation. "Nor am I expecting this to bring instant peace when you all have endured so many years of terror."

The animals involuntarily shiver in silence.

"However, I have put a lot of thought into this and hope it will be the stepping stone to the life of peace and plenty we all deserve to live."

Everyone in the crowd is too stunned to react immediately, and so for the first few seconds after the King's presentation, there is total silence. Even the crickets that produce constant ambience to the atmosphere with their trained bands are completely silent.

That is, until Dermacus, the large grey elephant, raises his trunk into the air and lets out a melodious trumpet in support of the King. Gradually, other elephants join in until there are supportive trumpets and loud chants of "God bless the King!" all around the Glebel.

The only difference between now and the other reigns the animals have experienced is that for the first time in nearly a century, they actually mean it.

Al, who is now sitting solemnly at the base of the neem tree, smiles at the jubilation.

His time has come, after all — he can feel the hands of his ancestors gently holding his hand and guiding him toward the oak tree where he can meet his family once more.

Al rests his head on the base of the neem tree that has shaded him since he was a child, shaded his mother, his mother's mother and many generations before him.

"God bless the new King." Al, the old chimpanzee says, and by the time the animals realise that the smile on his face isn't from a dream he can wake up from, he is already reunited with his family on the great oak tree that holds them all.

*   *   *

"You know, we are in danger if none of you chittering fools have realised it yet." Jerome says, feeling like the only one in his clan left with common sense.

The rest of the Royalists look up at him with grim looks on their bald, narrow faces. "We do not deny that," Pedro says, the squirrel skull necklace around his bald neck dangling loosely. "What we are saying is that there is nothing we can do."

Jerome scoffs and paces around the cave they have been hiding out in for the past year.

"So we just wait around for the lowlifes to lynch us up on stakes?" Jerome asks, exasperated at how his clan has chosen to sit around for death to take us. "Dare I remind you all that we used to rule over those scums? We used to have power—"

"But we don't anymore, Jer!" Pedro bellows, as exasperated as Jerome is feeling. "We no longer have that power, and even if there's no official announcement about the King letting go of our services, it's just a matter of time before the animals realise that."

Jerome and Pedro are having a face-off at this point, and the rest of the clan shift around nervously, not quite sure what to say.

"Maybe it's time to let go of the glory days, Jer," Pedro says. "Try and find favour once more with the—"

"There is no way I am going to pretend to be one of those lowlifes." Jerome scoffs, turning away from Pedro and pacing once more. "And you really think that they are going to welcome us with open arms? After all, what power did our ancestors hold over them? Power that we barely got to wield before that... imposter ascended the throne."

"Jero—"

"With this ridiculous plan to establish a court of law, we would probably be tried and sent to rot in the darkest corners of the dungeons." Jerome sneers. "Or maybe even sent into exile."

Pedro sighs, "So. What's your plan now?"

Jerome flaps his wing once, then he heads out to the mouth of the cave, tucked into a hidden spot at one of the highest mountains on the outskirts of Yakko forest. He can

still make out sounds of the jubilation that has carried on through the night.

"Now? We lie low and wait," Jerome says. "There will be an opportunity for us to rise back to what we once were."

Chapter Three

*I*t takes a productive number of years for the city-state of Dungalo to start coming into realisation and a couple more for the animals to find their footing in this new reality.

During the time it took to build the city-state, King Migag II launched programmes to better equip the animals, and the most significant ones were the judges and juries and lawyers trained on a newly drawn-up constitution.

The animals were seemingly well-adjusted throughout the whole process, and of all the effects, the most profound of all, observed Mr Hakkas, the social commentary podcaster, is certainly the way the children of the animals started knowing dreams once more.

In the past reigns of the cruel kings, no one had the courage to dream. They were more concerned about surviving the next hour without being dead. Ask an animal about their dreams in the reigns of that dark era, and they would ask you if that was a new trick question to see who was plotting against royalty — because only the brave dared to dream.

However, in the new city-state of Dungalo, you can now gently pull aside a young animal to ask the same question, and you would hear things like being a lawyer, a diplomat or a social commentator. These are the careers that gained popularity in the past few years of building the Dungalo city-state, and there are even more coming up — like the esteemed tech researchers and inventors that discover new technology to make the lives of the Dungalo animals easier.

The animals have never felt this much peace and order, that is for sure. And even if it was unsettling at first, as they kept expecting King Migag II to finally reveal a loophole to this whole plan that would dunk them back into even more terror.

It never happened, and so the animals allowed themselves to relax. Allowed themselves to explore further than the environment they'd been trapped in for so long, even if none had the desire now to leave Dungalo for good.

Dungalo is the envy of other neighbouring kingdoms, and people now fight to get in, not out, but with the whole citizenship system now set up, it's a bit hard for other kingdom animals to try and set up permanent residence.

On a chilly Tuesday evening, the animals of Dungalo are summoned to the Glebel on a rare occasion.

There hasn't been much need to frequent the Glebel, for the tech researchers have connected radios directly to the Royal Palace, where the King can speak to his people from the comfort of his palace to the comfort of their own homes.

So it's a bit surprising — if not inconvenient, as many complained — that they would be summoned to the Glebel on a cold evening.

The King is already seated on his throne by the time most animals arrive at the Glebel, his Queen and Prince by his sides.

King Migag II and Queen Sheila seem to be giving in to the natural ageing process. However, Prince Edgar is now a fully grown lion with a confidence about him that sets him apart from the meek lion cub he used to be. Everyone already speaks of what a great King he would be, especially since he's so involved in their kingdom with both charities and community service.

The Royals aren't the only ones that went through change. The Glebel is different now; it is no longer an open space but a massive hall set up with powerful speakers and microphones.

As soon as the hall seems to be at full capacity, the King stands to go to the lone microphone on the stage. His gait is slower, and the shine in his mane, while still maintained, seems to be losing its shine.

He starts to speak into the microphone, but a loud mechanical screech erupts from the speakers, and everyone shrinks back, covering their ears and cursing out loud.

The King looks up and fixes a stare at the top room where the technical team is currently operating. The monkeys—former message relayers—all scramble around to make some fixes. Soon after, one gives a bow to the King to let him know that it's okay to continue.

King Migag II looks back to his people and clears his throat.

"I know you all wonder why I have called you to the city square when I can speak to you through your radios," the King said. "Truth is, although the technology brought to us by our brilliant inventors has made our lives easier, I am starting to feel a disconnect among us that rely solely on these technologies and less on their neighbours."

Some of the older animals in the crowd

aggressively nod in agreement while side-eyeing their younger ones. Even if the technology introduced to the people of

Dungalo was initially welcomed with open arms by a good majority of animals, over time there started to be loud, diverse opinions about it.

The older animals complained of the loss of a sense of community, especially in the younger generation that would rather rely on robots to get tasks done.

The younger animals accused the older generation of being scared and

close-minded to better change and innovation because they unknowingly glorified the suffering of their days.

However, with the King agreeing with their sentiments, the older animals were feeling rather smug.

"I prefer to be in the presence of my people when I speak to them," King Migag II continued. "Not in a cold, technical room alone speaking into a strangely shaped microphone."

Behind the King, people could see Prince Edgar visibly sigh like he'd heard these particular words over and over again. He's part of the younger generation, anyway.

"The reason I have called you all here is to

implement a change that has long been needed for this new world we live in now," the King says, to the uneasy murmurs of the animals.

The older generation is gripped by fear, hoping that their fears that the idea of Dungalo is a trap are not about to manifest now, after things have been so peaceful for so long. Even if they relaxed after a while, the uneasiness never fully left, with the trauma from the dark eras never giving them peace.

However, King Migag II soon calms their mind.

"Ever since Dungalo has evolved from our minds into the greatness we see today, there have been very minimal reports of the cruel human race hurting us."

The animals' loud cheer loudly erupts in the Glebel for the king, needing to be calmed down after a while to let him continue speaking.

"This is credit to us all," King Migag II continues, voice raspy. "To our vigilance and patriotism to the city-state of Dungalo." He pauses to catch a breath. "And of course, major credit goes to the Royal guards that have been stationed within and without the walls of Dungalo."

The King nods to the Royal Gorilla Guards stationed strategically around the hall.

They stamp the end of their spears down in respect to the king.

"I am immensely blessed to have such loyal and wonderful subjects, indeed." King Migag II says, with a little bow of his head. "Thank you for doing your best to help create a beautiful world for us all."

"All hail the great King!" a young Chimp from the crowd shouts, and everyone soon joins in the chant.

King Migag II lets them go on for a little while before signalling for their attention once more.

"Yes, the Royal Guards have been doing a spectacular job in protecting us," he says, solemn. "But as our state and our reputation grow, so will our enemies. Which is why I discussed with the head of the Royal Guard to come to the decision of creating a new branch of security — the Royal Police Force."

The animals cheer, seemingly taken by whatever King Migag II says. He has created a life of so much peace and progress for them that it is nearly impossible to be against him. And even if it isn't the case, who can ever disregard the idea of more security that'll make their daily lives even safer? Or the idea of more job openings?

Many animals start imagining their lives as a member of the Royal Police Force. There would be great perks, definitely; working directly under the royal family would definitely guarantee a comfortable life. Every animal wanted that.

"There will be conditions, however," the King says, barrelling through the fantasies of a great deal of excited animals. "We need one species of animal to guarantee

peaceful cooperation. This species also needs to be very agile and light on their feet to quickly alert fellow animals about dangers, as well as have great eyesight to scout the enemies better."

Animals like the sloths and the moles quickly deflate, and along with them, their dreams of a more comfortable life.

"They also have to be big enough to withstand confrontation, if any."

There is instant murmuring, both of satisfaction and disappointment at the conditions. Little critters like the foxes and hedgehogs and meerkats and squirrels and all are quickly discouraged by the size requirement.

A good majority of animals that are more focused on their protection eventually agree that this is a fair condition.

"I will be personally approving every group that would be interested in this role." King

Migag II starts to conclude. "Long live the citizens of Dungalo."

"Long live the King!"

Chapter Four

*A*mongst the animals, there is usually a peaceful co-existence among the various species, especially since they realise being united is the best way to resist their common, cruel enemy — the human race.

So they all made interaction with each other an important part of their daily lives, with some different species even forming lifelong bonds with each other.

However, at the end of the day, you would usually find species of the same kind hanging around each other as they retired for the day. Most of the time, they intermingled with other species that are similar to them or that share certain struggles with them.

This is the same for the little critters, who aren't taken too seriously amongst the animals. Not exactly maliciously or in a condescending manner, but if you look too closely, you realise just how often they're brushed off.

The critters are used to this, only because they don't realise they're getting used to a pattern that treats them as such. It's a normal thing they don't seem to have a problem with because, of course, there is always going to be a ranking system. And they are not exactly at the top of it.

Moreover, they managed to produce an important societal figure in the years Dungalo was being built. There isn't an animal that isn't familiar with Barr. Jones, the brilliant lawyer and the best seen since the establishment of the Dungalo constitution.

And so the little critters are content with living a life of minimal ambition. Until the night King Migag II announced the plans for a new security force.

While heading back to their section of Dungalo — the one majorly populated by the little critters — after the meeting with the King, they come across members of a clan almost long forgotten because of how scarce their appearance has been in the past years.

They come across Royalists.

Zainab, the hedgehog trader, is the first to spot them conversing by the side of the boulevard they're passing through. She alerts the others to their presence, and it's only a couple of them that feel the involuntary fear of spotting a royalist. The others were either too young at the peak of the Royalists' reign and couldn't remember much of that fear. Some just hadn't been born yet.

However, they did hear the tales of the wrinkly, bald creatures with the long necks that would make you and your family disappear if you so much as breathe wrong in their direction. And it's the first time seeing them for some of them.

The conversing Royalists don't seem to have noticed them yet, and the little critters are still undecided on what to do when they tune into their conversation.

"The King is meant to foster a community that allows his citizens to participate and prove that they also have what it takes," the Royalist with a shrunken skull necklace says. "Not one that oppresses the ones that try to contribute. It's heartbreaking."

"You're right, brother," replies the other royalist sadly, with a shake of his especially bald neck and head. "Like the poor little critters. I see how unfairly these honest animals are treated like second-class citizens."

"Less than that!" The skull-necklace wielder opposed with a heated determination to call out injustice. "The other day, I was by the market and saw one of the little critters continuously talked over when they tried to contribute to a trader's meeting."

Zainab's ear perks up.

"This poor thing was trying to make a valuable point! But what happened?" The royalist continued, looking continuously enraged. "She kept getting talked over, but five minutes later, a jaguar makes the same point and is hailed for it."

Zain grits her little teeth as she remembers when this, indeed, did happen to her.

During the quarterly traders' meeting, the trader animals were looking for a solution to the longstanding problem of missing or mixed-up packages.

Before the building of Dungalo, animals had limited their trading to just within Yakko Forest, as they had not been allowed to leave the borders. But with King Migag II and the building of Dungalo, inter-kingdom trading had blown up, and the animals of Dungalo became the first to expand trading to the other kingdoms, near and far.

However, the problem of package mix-ups

still remained, and, worse, when it went missing, there wasn't a way to trace it back to the owner. Even if someone's name had been on it, the trading world was too vast to start tracking down one person. It was too much of a hassle.

Zainab, however, did have a solution that she'd been turning over in her mind for a while.

Seals.

"W-what about official individual s-seals?" Zainab had stammered, for she'd always been a timid one with a fear of public speaking. However, the animals had continued stressing about the problem like she'd never spoken.

Zainab had continued, for she believed that if she kept talking, someone would take notice. "W-we can all assign individual seals to r-registered traders..." The animals kept talking over her. "To make it easier to track down, m-maybe we should have different trading c-clans. Where each member is registered." Zain had looked around for some validation, feeling her short-term confidence waver, but she'd continued. "T-there should be clan embassies in other Kingdoms as well... I-I can volunteer to be in the team that discusses this with the Kingdoms."

At this point, Greg the Hyena had let out a little giggle, as if he found the idea of Zainab making deals with other kingdoms hilarious. Some other animals chuckled as well, but subtly enough to make Zainab wonder if it was actually at her or something else.

No one responded to Zainab, and she'd shrunk back but still with the fire of determination in her heart. She was going to request an audience with the King to present this idea. Yes. She knew that something great would come out of it, and if she wasn't paid heed here, she knew the kind King would listen to her.

So Zainab kept quiet and sat back, planning to head to the royal palace immediately after the meeting.

However, less than ten minutes later, Ali, the Jaguar, suggested the exact same thing.

"Right now, I think our problem stems from operating solo." Ali had said, with everyone's attention on him. "We have these traders' meetings, but at the end of the day, there's no official registry for the traders."

It had started slightly different enough that Zainab had no suspicions; however, the more Ali spoke, the more Zainab was appalled at how blatantly her idea had been stolen.

"We can create a few trading clans based on usual travel routes, and each clan can have their own seal as well." Ali looked increasingly smug the more he spoke. "When packages are sent out, individual and clan seals can be put on them. It makes it easier to trace back to the trading clan, then the individual."

"That *issssss* brilliant!" Denis, the cobra had hissed out his support and other animal traders quickly joined in.

At first, Zainab had been too stunned to make any comment, but she, enraged, soon tried to fight for her idea. This time, she wasn't ignored, but it wasn't the kind of attention she'd wanted because the traders started saying how it was cute that she thought she could come up with that idea. Some said they never heard her speak throughout the meeting, including Greg, who still seemed to be laughing at Zainab. Some asked her to calm down and stop making a scene.

The only ones who had tried to support her were the other little critters who were as timid as she was and didn't initially try to defend her. But the more they watched someone close to them get trampled over, the more they forced themselves to find their voices.

But as usual, their words were laughed at like they were the ones being silly.

The injustice Zainab felt was deepened when, a mere few days later, she heard that King Migag

II had presented Ali a recognition award for his innovative idea and made him the overseer of the whole trading expansion project.

Right now, Ali lived in a reserved area of Dungalo where those recognised by the King are given luxurious residences as well as a monthly supply of food sponsored by the King.

The thought that she could've had that and elevated her family's lifestyle but it'd been stolen from her still enraged her. It'd been some time since then, and Zainab had chosen to move on since she knew it would be a lost battle if she continued to fight for it.

However, the words of the royalists now brought back that sense of injustice she'd felt.

"I hope the little critters start to make their voices heard more," the very bald royalist says. "Especially now the King has deliberately excluded them from being nominated for the security force. We all know that he gave a requirement that would particularly benefit the big cats, ignoring the strengths other species provide."

And with one final flap and without seeming to notice the group of critters, the Royalist spread their massive wings and flap away, flying back into the sky and leaving the critters pondering over their words.

*   *   *

Pedro and Jerome perch on a tree where they can't be easily spotted unless searched for.

Together, they stare at the little critters standing in the middle of the boulevard, discussing. Before continuing their journey back to their section of Dungalo, their discussion gets a bit more passionate, full of fire.

Jerome smirks deviously as he watches them go.

"And now, brother," he says, eyes still trained on the little critters and Zain, who seems to be at the lead of the discussion. "It begins."

*   *   *

On Thursday morning, news of the little critters holding a massive protest in front of the palace of the King spreads everywhere.

The problem with the critters is that, even if they are often brushed aside as often as one breathes, their combined numbers rival every other species of animal. And so, having every single one of the critters protest is a significant event.

Especially since it's been a long, long time since any protest has been held in both the old kingdom of Yakko Forest and the new city-state of Dungalo.

They all hold placards, demanding a fair state of Dungalo that also favours the little critters, with emphasis on the King stopping the discrimination that discouraged the critters from participating in the security force.

A few animals did try to stop them when the protest began, convinced that it's another foolish tactic of the timid little critters that cried about injustice every market day. The other animals are used to getting a little critter to back down from whatever they considered foolishness. It doesn't work this time, because after years of being forced to endure injustice and being made to believe it was normal, the critters are fed up.

When word reaches King Migag II in the royal palace about the protest, he is shocked. Mostly because this is the very first time in his reign as king that there is a collective disagreement targeted at him.

This causes a deep uneasiness within him, and for the first time in his reign as king, he feels fear. Fear that he is a terrible king and might end up like his predecessors.

And there is nothing King Migag II fears

more than being perceived as a cruel, unreasonable king like his father and father's father and a good number of his ancestors were.

For the first time, King Migag II chose to hide away, in fear of having these thoughts about himself confirmed. So he ignores the protest of the little critters on the first day to retreat into a silent reflection.

On the second day of the protest, the little critters are still ignored. As well as the third day.

And now the animals of Dungalo start to wonder. Even if a good majority of them think the little critters are being ungrateful and dramatic, the King ignoring the little critters makes them start to wonder if he actually cares about the concerns of his people.

There is a sudden division of opinions among the city-state of Dungalo, and for the first time since the crowning of King Migag II, they feel real uneasiness. One that has them wondering if now would be a good time to flee the state in case the King turns out to be playing the long game to gain their trust, then trap them once more.

It is during all the uneasiness that another rumour starts spreading: the king has always had the Cheetahs in mind for the position in the security force.

This is a bad, bad sign for the animals.

For everyone knew how easily corruptible the Cheetahs are and if the animals rely on them to protect them from the humans, who's to say the corrupt cats won't sell them out when offered something good enough to appease their greed?

Like one instance where the trade lawyer had taken bribes from another trader cheetah who everyone knew poached Yvonne the orangutan's goods and sold them as his. Yvonne had taken him to court but her lawyer wasn't as cunning as Joe's own lawyer.

Everyone knows the cheetahs are bad news and are assuming that King Migag II is aware of this fact as well. If it had been before the whole little critters protested, the animals would have given King Migag II the benefit of the doubt.

However, with so much uneasiness going around Dungalo and the King's radio silence, some people believe it instantly.

On the fourth day, a sit-at-home order is issued to every animal and King Migag II breaks his silence through the radio.

"I have been made aware of what has been going on in Dungalo and it breaks my heart to see my people going through so much pain," King Migag II says, straight to the point. "I am here to assure you that as your King, it is my responsibility to foster an environment where every animal feels seen and heard. That has always been my goal since I took up a different mantle from my predecessors."

There is a long pause and all the animals can hear is the King's breathing, a bit unsteady.

"Let it also be known that I would never show a particular kind of bias that would strip any animal of their right to use their own voice." He pauses briefly. "And so, if it makes my subjects happy, I will be leaving the whole process of picking a security force to protect you in your hands. Because I believe you all know what is best for you."

And with that, the radio goes static.

*   *   *

While the little critters feel that the king did not directly address them in his vague statement, they are still appeased that the condition for the security force has been lifted.

However, this time, the distaste of the animals for the little critters is no longer hidden. They are blamed for all the uneasiness that has been going on in Dungalo; shunned for being ungrateful and making an issue out of nothing.

Some animals go as far as not patronising any little critter business out of sheer spite.

Yet, despite all this, a critter species makes it to the final round of the voting process that the animals have set up for the picking of the security force species.

This species is the meerkat clan and they are up against the cheetahs.

A lot of animals oppose this, wondering how two of the most disliked species in Dungalo made it to the final round. A lot of animals accuse the system of being rigged.

But no one does this loudly, not wanting to create a situation where the fire is turned on them like it currently is on the little critters.

And so they move forward with gritted teeth.

The whole process of nomination and the first voting round takes a couple of months. And for the final voting round, a time gap is given for animals to carefully make their decision.

Although the decision is tough, it might have been made easier the week before the final elections.

During a press conference to pledge their commitment to this cause, Dom, the leading representative for the Cheetahs' party, makes a smug, insensitive comment that throws off even the supporters the Cheetahs had managed to gain.

A reporter had asked him about his confidence in the Cheetahs' victory and Dom had replied,

"Of course the Cheetahs will win; we are a far more superior species than the little critters."

This makes headlines in the animal papers about how the Cheetahs think they are better than every other animal.

Supporters start throwing out and burning the merch they'd gotten in support of the Cheetahs. Social commentators start digging deep into the psyche of Dom and the Cheetahs, with one noting that it would take a certain type of narcissistic disorder to believe that was an appropriate thing to say and still expect support.

Even during the plays that occasionally take place in the Glebel for the entertainment of animals, they start making parodies of that moment.

Slowly, the Cheetahs lose their popularity, and now, all attention is on the meerkats. Out of sheer spite, some animals turn to supporting the meerkats. To show the

Cheetahs that no matter what kind of high horse they are on, the support of the general public is still the greatest asset they just lost.

The Cheetahs changed their representative and tried to do some damage control when they saw just how much Dom's comment had rubbed the animals the wrong way.

They engage in free vigilante activities across Dungalo, make a public apology to the animals of Dungalo; have their new representative personally apologise to the meerkats.

But alas, it is too late.

For when the election day comes, and by the end of it, news reaches every animal of Dungalo through their radios.

The meerkats won.

Chapter Five

The meerkats' clan victory as the new security force isn't really celebrated, except by the critters who are proud to have new representatives in higher places.

Some animals of Dungalo are still a bit miffed that they had to support the critters because the only other option was worse. So even if they gave their votes, they still feel robbed of a choice they would've wanted (which would have been species of their own kind, really). But there's nothing to do at this point.

This is not to say that there aren't some animals that truly support the meerkats. There are, and in good majority as well. Especially the ones that do not care for any forced narrative of a species being an enemy.

Or those that actually recognise the meerkats to be a perfect fit for their security force.

"When you think about it, meerkats are fast—maybe not more than Cheetahs—but they are small, and that makes them tricky to catch, so they would not be deterred by enemies from alerting the animals to danger." Farouk, the horse and social commentator, observed. "Although I still wish that the horses had made it to the final round—we do fit the criteria perfectly and also have excellent hearing as a bonus."

The support of the true meerkat supporters grows louder after this, and they start defending the meerkats when they are opposed in public.

During all the divide and siding amongst the citizens of Dungalo, the meerkats are preparing to have a congratulatory banquet with the King.

They actually didn't believe they would have come this far, only being nominated by the little critters to represent them so a point could be proven.

With the aggressive support of the little critters and allies, they were up against the Cheetahs which, despite their terrible reputation, seemed to be the popular choice of the animals.

Only because of sheer luck brought about by the comment of Dom, were they able to win.

And a win for the meerkats is a win for all the little critters that want to prove they can also do great things. For the young, little critters who can now dare to dream as big as they want to.

This is a historical moment being made, and there's nothing as fulfilling as it is.

Yet there is still fear amongst the meerkat clan, for they know how great of a responsibility the security of Dungalo is, and it has been thrust upon them.

And even if they were nominated in the first place because they had some great ideas, it's still terrifying to know that a whole city-state relies on you for their protection. And with the recent growing distaste for the little critters, this is a critical situation where they have to prove themselves over and over.

On the day of the celebratory royal banquet, the meerkat clan receive blessings from the little critters' community and meet King Migag II at the royal palace.

The meerkats are nervous, worried that the King might also share the sentiments of his subjects about the little critters being the cause of the divide and uneasiness in Dungalo.

However, the King's reception of them is filled with nothing but warmth and interest in the latest Royal staff.

The meerkats are fed and entertained with a play, and right before the end, King Migag II makes eye contact with the elected commander-in-chief of the meerkats, Commander Jay. It is time to discuss the security plans for Dungalo.

Commander Jay bows slightly and pitter-patters to the King's side.

"Why don't we take a stroll through the gardens?" King Migag II suggests taking the lead. "Let's hear your plans."

Commander Jay is animated as he tells King Migag II of the meerkats security plans for Dungalo, showing just how much thought he and the meerkats have put into this.

From alarm cries to military training and watch towers tall enough for the meerkats to make up for their small size.

"Although our small size is also a great advantage for spy missions," Commander Jay says at some point. "For dark shadow missions where we can infiltrate enemy territory. It's risky, but that's what we'll be trained to do."

It takes a good number of hours before King Migag II and Commander Jay are back from their stroll through the Royal Gardens, with King Migag II fully briefed on everything. There had been some doubts earlier, when King Migag II heard that meerkats -- from the critters community -- had won the security force elections.

There had been doubts, indeed. However,

the meerkats have now proved that they have every right to be in that position.

For what is seen as a disadvantage, they turn into an advantage—like using the small size to infiltrate enemy communities.

As well as providing ideas to strengthen those weak points—the tall watchtowers and enlisting the help of nocturnal creatures to help scout at night.

King Migag II is especially marvelled at the meerkats' ideas to always be prepared for war because of the suspicious silence from the side of the humans. Commander Jay says the meerkats believe it's only the silence before the storm and that it would never hurt to come up with strategies to ensure that animals have the upper hand if it ever comes to that.

All in all, the meerkats' preparedness and ideas are impressive, and especially so to King Migag II because they don't plan to hoard all this newfound power to themselves.

They actually have plans to enlist the help of other animals with strengths they can borrow from.

Not only from the nocturnals for their exceptional night sight. Commander Jay also mentioned having the primates train the security force because of their martial arts skills and having the porcupines and snails and a good number of other animals provide materials they need for setting enemy traps.

All signs point to the fact that the interest of Dungalo is at heart, and it is not just a plan to accumulate power that might be turned to the oppression reminiscent of his forefather's days. King Migag II wants no hand in any situation that would bring back the tyranny he worked so hard to eliminate.

And so, addressing the rest of the meerkats in the great royal hall, his words are simple but full of support.

"I, King Migag the second, will always stand by the meerkats for as long as you have the interest of Dungalo at heart."

That evening, shocking news spread about Dungalo.

King Migag II has raised the societal ranks of the meerkats to second.

A monumental shift, given that this means that after answering to the Royal Family, the citizens of Dungalo are also obligated to pay a similar respect to the meerkats, even without the command of the King.

This position was previously held by the tigers, who are nobles in the royal kingdom and have done quite a significant amount of philanthropic work.

So it is quite a shock that the meerkats — *little critters!* — have been promoted to second to the King, as a perk for securing the security force role.

Not a lot of animals are happy about this, mostly due to their egos and refusing to answer to a little critter.

Although King Migag II meant quite well to give the meerkats as few roadblocks as possible in creating a safer and more secure Dungalo, he'd unknowingly contributed to an already brewing storm.

One that would break the already pulsing silence with the force of a thousand lightnings.

Chapter Six

*D*uring the dark eras of former Kings, the outskirts of Yakko Forest were a terrible place to be—and not only because you might've gotten accused of escape if spotted by a Royalist or a devoted follower and had your family mysteriously disappear.

There was also the threat of humans always staying hidden or laying deathly traps around those parts, in wait for the unfortunate animal that stumbled across them.

During the building of Dungalo, however, some bigger animals that would be less susceptible to the trickery of humans were tasked with scouting the area and protecting the smaller animals who checked for traps.

The animals had quickly discovered that humans were cowards who would back away when there was a large group of animals. It was this way they were able to reform the outskirts of Yakko Forest into something safer and had extended the aerial watch of the crows to those parts.

But even after that, only a few animals are brave enough to approach the outskirts that have birthed so much terror and bad memories.

It is on these same outskirts that three Tigers are strolling leisurely.

Even before the reign of King Migag II, Tigers have always been fearless animals and would occasionally come here without fear of humans.

This might have been due to their privilege of being distantly related to the throne that had a deal with the humans. It might have also been a sense of confidence in their power over humans — as long as it wasn't an orchestrated attack.

Whichever it was — *is* — the Tigers have never had any real reason to fear humans.

Especially since a Tiger was the first witnessed animal to bravely launch at three armed humans. He'd come out with some gunshot injuries, but none of the attacking humans had survived the Tiger.

Perhaps it was from that day that Tigers had amassed even more respect — and in an era where the animals had zero respect but a lot of fear in the presence of the Lion Kings, the Tigers were the first ones to truly gain the respect and loyalty of most animals.

This caused the Lions to grow a terrible disdain for them, because they saw the hooded glimpses of how much the animals would gladly tune to whichever melody the Tigers needed them to play—while they had to instigate terror first before getting anyone to do their bidding.

Not that the Tigers really cared for any of this, for they have always been solitary animals without a sense of community. As long as they are never disturbed, they never pay mind to matters around them.

And the only reason the lions never tried to do anything rash to the Tigers was because they benefited from their presence. The wickedness of the past reign of Lions made them not trust any creature they worked with—not the Royalists carrying out the dirty work nor the humans providing the Lions with the fear factor they needed to keep their subjects in check, in return for unrestricted capturing of whatever animals they needed.

The past Lions feared that betrayal could come at any moment by those they worked with, so they needed to have that illusion of a relationship with the Tigers intact.

Because no one dared mess with the Tigers or

anyone associated with the Tigers in fear of retaliation.

It's been a long time since the dark era, and things are no longer the same, though. With the deal with humans long severed and the Royalist services let go of, King

Migag II has no betrayal to fear and in turn doesn't need leverage to keep that betrayal at bay.

The animals love him and respect him the same way the Tigers had been respected during the dark era, and the current Royal Family is now the leader the then oppressed animals had wished the Tigers to become, to the displeasure of the Tigers now.

See, the Tigers never took the throne because they held a satisfaction of still holding more power over the Lions despite not being on the throne. There's a perverse feeling of power that comes from knowing you are more revered than the ones supposedly ranked higher than you.

That feeling had been enough for the Tigers, but these days, no one respected any animal more than they did King Migag II and the current Royal Family. The Tigers had long since lost grip of that power.

And now, they've been thrown off their 2nd societal ranking by... *little critters!*

"We wouldn't be going through this if Great Grandfather had just taken the throne when he had the chance."

The three Tigers strolling through the outskirts are directly related brothers and the great-grandchildren of the one Tiger that annihilated three humans that overstepped their boundaries.

The one that just spoke is Meevo, the youngest of the three that doesn't have the pretence of not wanting power, like the other Tigers seem to have to keep up their nonchalant attitudes.

"We do not concern ourselves with these matters, Meev." Mario, the oldest sibling, says. "Politics is not for the Tigers—we're too noble for that."

Meevo rolls his eyes with an annoyed growl. "Oh, give me a break. We're so noble that we've been pushed down one spot in society."

"Meevo—" Raymond, the middle sibling, starts but is cut off by Meevo's continued rant.

"It's just one spot now, but if we keep up with this, we might even find ourselves below the worms of the earth!" Meevo glances between his two brothers. "Do you not

understand the severity of this? The animals are starting to think that we're pushovers, that—"

"That is enough, Meevo!" Mario roars, obviously swayed by his brother's words but still adamant on keeping the image he's been raised with. "Our clan has no interest in the throne. That is the end of this matter."

Meevo is not done, as he's one who never knows when to stop. Raymond notices the lit fire in his eyes and gives Meevo a warning glare, which is ignored.

"Brother—"

"You know the boy has a point, don't you think?"

The three brothers stop in their tracks and perk up their ears for the source of the sound. A shadow flies over them, and they all look up to see a massive vulture circling overhead. It's Pedro, the Royalist.

"I am an old vulture now, but I was but a wee lad when your great grandfather was the talk of Yakko Forest. The majestic Tharros who showed the enemy that he was not one to be messed with."

"We do not interact with traitors." Mario bellows. "Find your way, bird." "Traitors?" Pedro asks curiously, perching on a high tree that guarantees safety

from a Tiger's tall leap. "I know of the reputation we've had and still have, but I assure you—we were only pawns in this cruel game. Made to carry all the blame and tossed aside for the animals to tread on when convenient."

"Ignore him." Raymond says and urges an intrigued Meevo to keep walking. Mario snarls at Pedro, which startles him enough to fly over to a higher tree.

"But none about me and more about the great Tiger clan." Pedro says as Mario follows after his brothers. "Just a generation ago, the animals were willing to follow the Tigers wherever they led them to."

"Go away while we're still nice." Raymond says, a quiet threat in his usually non-confrontational tone.

"I do not come to look for trouble. I would never dare to mess with the Kings that never needed a crown." Pedro smirks, a bait in his tone. "I'm only here to remind you of the days when even the Lions feared your clan; revered you and depended on you to protect the illusion of power they had.

"When the animals would gladly drop all that they had to follow the ones they truly considered King."

Meevo stops walking and turns to Pedro who's flying high tree to high tree to keep up with the brothers.

"Keep walking, Meevo." Mario growls but is ignored by his younger brother. "*Meevo!*"

"I am a traitor, I admit." Pedro continues. "It is barely my fault that I am this way. It was what I was taught, and I knew no better than to follow in the footsteps of my clan. I had no choice."

"You always had a choice to resist!" Mario snarls back at Pedro, who perches on a higher tree than the one he previously occupied. However, he seems satisfied. Smug, even.

"You're right." Pedro smirks. "We all have a choice to resist. You have a choice to resist this topple of order. You claim not to care about power, but do you really not?"

"We do not need to drag for the throne to gain power." Mario seethes.

"Who said you needed to drag for the throne?" Pedro asks, raising a bald eyebrow. "The reign of the Lions is coming to an end, undone by none other than the King that claims to bring better change."

"What are you saying?" Meevo asks.

"The King is weak, is all I say. Too cowardly to make decisions by himself." Pedro says, tone laced with venom. "He leaves the hard work to the animals and takes all the credit. And every animal is blind to this deceit because they are being tossed a scrap of what they've always dreamt of — freedom. But it's all a farce!"

"Why should we listen to you? Your clan is a big part of the reason the animals jump at these *scraps*, as you put it." Raymond cuts in. "We never fully experienced the height of it, but weren't you Royalists the ones caging animals in the reality they were tricked into?"

"I am one of the last of the Royalists from the dark eras." Pedro admits, bowing his long neck. "I did unspeakable things, yes — all under orders. If anyone is to be punished, I am."

"Of course you are." Raymond snips.

"However, the generation after me is innocent." Pedro says, venomous anger slipping into his tone. "If the King is truly as fair as he thinks he is, he should realise this and let us integrate freely back into society."

"No one pushed you out in the first place." Mario points out. "You went into hiding on your own accord."

"Is that what they're telling every animal?" Pedro asks, and the brothers go into stunned silence.

Admittedly, nothing was said about the disappearance of the Royalists since King Migag II's crowning. The animals might've wondered where they went, but no one was particularly curious enough to know about the symbols of the dark eras.

Over time, the Royalists became a distant memory, one that got washed away in the tide of a better change. Maybe just like how the former position of the tigers is now slowly being washed out.

"We're all pawns in the game of the Lions," Pedro continues. "The vultures were unfortunate enough to be used long enough to start looking like knights. And when it was convenient, we were discarded with the narratives of villains."

Beady eyes lock with Mario's fierce one.

"You said it; we all have a choice to resist being pawns." "We're not pawns." Raymond seethes.

"Pawns usually don't recognise when they are just that." Pedro says. "But having that trait bloodline-deep, I'm fairly confident in my ability to recognise the patterns—feeling safe and giving your trust, and when you realise it's a trap, it's too late. How do you think the dark eras started?"

Pedro spreads his wings, and a tiny scroll falls out, dropping to the ground and rolling to Meevo's paws.

"We all have a choice." Pedro says, launching into the air and circling above the tigers, casting shadows. "And silence is also a choice that can crumble great clans."

The vulture's shadow glides over the brothers one more time before vanishing into the trees, leaving them staring at the scroll like a trap with its pin already pulled.

Chapter Seven

*D*ifferent animals are gathered in a dim room and discussing in hush tones with their kinds.

In a corner by the door, Jerome and Pedro stand side by side as they watch the interactions and occasional distrusting glances among the different species of big cats— except for the Lions... and the Tigers.

"You said they would be here." A Cheetah snarls at the Royalists. "As much as I hate to admit it, we need the Tigers on our side to have a reputable case."

"Don't loop us into your untrustworthiness." A Jaguar snarls back at the Cheetah that just spoke. "The only disadvantage we have, even with the Tigers on our side, is being associated with the tricky Cheetahs... why were they even invited here?"

"Why don't you shut up?" Another Cheetah

snarls back, and then chaos ensues.

Pedro and Jerome sigh and look at each other, wondering why these are the species the animals consider top of societal rankings. Pedro is about to say something when a low growl reverberates around the room, shutting up the big cats instantly.

The tigers are here.

Mario, Raymond, Meevo and a select group of other Tigers from their clan strut into the room with an aura of elegance about them. They don't say a word, but the other cats immediately clear away, making space for them at the front and not minding if they are squeezed into the very back.

Once the Tigers are settled, Mario growls at the Royalists. "Well?" Jerome jolts into action immediately. "We thank you all —"

"And straight to the point before we have second thoughts about coming here." Another Tiger growls.

Jerome gives a tight smile and bows in a way that can be interpreted as mocking. "Of course, my Lords. Pedro?"

Pedro takes the lead as Jerome slinks back into a corner to watch everything unfold.

"We have a solid case against the King, who has disrupted the natural order of the animals as well as put the lives of his subjects at risk over trying to be 'inclusive'." Pedro says. "Our lawyer will brief us further on the subject."

From a door on the side of the room, out walks Jones, the fox lawyer handling a pile of documents, and behind him, another vulture pushing a table out of the said room.

When it's positioned properly, Jones drops his papers orderly on it.

Barr. Jones has a very clean-cut appearance, with trimmed, polished fur with a matching orange moustache to go with it. As the big cats watch him, they start to feel very stifled by his very formal demeanour—even the tigers, who can be said to be very reserved in their attitude.

However, beyond the Fox's stifling appearance, there is something else—a glaring question all the big cats are thinking.

"First of all, we would need to gather the signatures of every big cat in this room to be compiled into a legal petition document." Barr. Jones jumps straight into the topic.

"You will also have to get the signatures of the rest of your clans and other species that you may have an advantage over and are willing – or obligated – to give their signatures. The goal is as many signatures as—"

"Aren't you a little critter?" A Lynx voices

the question everyone is thinking. "This is also a protest against the meerkats being unfit to protect this city. How do we trust someone who is betraying his own community?"

The big cats all murmur in agreement at the Lynx's words, but Barr. Jones is as calm and collected as ever as he assesses the situation. When the murmurs start dying down, Barr. Jones speaks.

"I only stand for what I believe is reasonable, not a forced concept of community." His tone is level as he speaks. "Truly, can any animal truly say that they believe the meerkats can protect this Dungalo we've worked so hard to protect, or that the King is not showing too much leniency as an overcompensation to not be accused of being discriminatory?"

There is a short stretch of silence until Pedro speaks with a saccharine drip to his voice.

"Shall we continue then? I'm sure we are all eager to hear about this."

And continue they did, with the big cats, the vultures and the fox talking carefully scheming ways to defame King Migag II and his rule.

*　　　*　　　*

A week after the meerkats are elected as

security force, a celebratory carnival is organised for them—mostly by the little critter community but also approved and supported by King Migag II.

The excitement is contagious, and even other animals not from the little critter community help in organising the carnival. Indeed, preparations for the carnival is one of the most unified things the citizens of Dungalo have ever done.

There are animals willingly volunteering their services, such as setting up booths and game structures or being a vendor for the event or organising the activities in order.

Observing the days leading up to the celebration, King Migag II is convinced that the meerkats are the right choice, for he wants nothing more than for all the animals to live in unity.

Even though the carnival date is in a tight time frame, because of the teamwork, the animals still manage to finish the preparations on time for the day.

In all this, the meerkats feel grateful but are still a bit shy of all the sudden attention they've been receiving for a while now. It's something they still have to get used to but are not sure if they ever fully can.

The day of the carnival comes, and the sun seems to be shining even brighter on that day. Before noon, the space outside the Glebel where the carnival structures are set up is already bustling.

Young animals are running around in groups, exploring the different activities and games that the carnival has to offer. Older animals settle themselves in food and drink tents, having civil discussions and polite disagreements.

With the way everything is progressing, all the animals are convinced that nothing would be able to spoil that mood. Before dusk, the meerkats would have a march that they've been practising for days, then give a rundown of their plans for Dungalo. And then King Migag II would give a speech.

The animals are actually starting to feel positive about the meerkats and are looking forward to hearing their security plans for Dungalo.

Things go well until after the meerkats' parade march, then the little hedgehog MC for the last part of the carnival lets the animals know that the floor is open for a few citizens of Dungalo to either showcase a talent or give a speech.

First up to go on stage is an elephant, who gives a waterworks trick with her trunk, to the delight of baby animals. Other animals who go up either sing badly out of tune or present a badly written poem to the King, which is still all in good fun.

That is, until the hedgehog receives a scroll offstage.

"Oh, this is presented to our King. God bless the King." the hedgehog bows towards the spacious tent closest to the stage where King Migag II and the rest of the royal family are occupying.

King Migag II motions him to carry on with it, believing the scroll is from an animal too shy to come present, maybe, or another badly written poem to him. It's all in good fun, he thinks.

However, as the hedgehog proceeds to roll open the scroll, his little face drops and he looks up, open-mouthed, at the King.

Animals are curious now, as well as King Migag II who sits up a bit straighter. "What is it?" he asks, and the hedgehog first glances around the crowd before

pitter-pattering to the King's tent and handing over the scroll.

"It's a court order, my Lord." the hedgehog says as quietly as he can but perhaps not quiet enough because one thing about the animals is that a good number of them have insanely great hearing.

And so, whispers of "court order" pass around the crowd, and now all eyes are on the King, who is, in his own right, shaken by whatever content he finds in the scroll.

Queen Sheila, who is as confused as the rest of the animals, stares curiously at her husband's still frame before gently taking the scroll from him. Then her own face falls before she whips her concerned gaze back to the still frozen King Migag II.

Prince Edgar looks curiously back and forth between his parents. "What is it?

What's in the scroll?"

Queen Sheila, without taking her concerned gaze away from her husband, says in a voice barely more than a whisper.

"Your father's worst nightmare."

Chapter Eight

*N*ews spread quickly among the citizens of Dungalo; King Migag II has been sued by the big cats and other species of animals (suspiciously in relation with the big cats) for being a terrible King to his subjects.

Of course, some animals find that notion ridiculous.

"If the King is terrible, then I move slow." Pablo, the Sloth had once said very heatedly in a marketside argument, efficiently halting the conversation.

"You do move slow, Pablo," the Zebra beside him had countered. "Oh yeah? Want to see how fast I can strike, huh? *Huh!?*"

Some animals, however, think it's a perfectly solid case against the King.

"I personally feel like the King has been getting a little weak recently," A Wolf had told the sheep acquaintance he'd made as they headed to the outskirts for a stroll together. "I think it might have something to do with old age. You do also think the King is getting old, don't you?"

While some animals did not want to involve themselves in the matter.

"It's not going to make any difference if we take a stand or not. Things will still unfold how they want to."

All in all, every animal in the city-state of Dungalo is tuned in to this first-in-history event of a King being sued by his people, and when the day for the court case came around, animals had to be coordinated by the royal guards.

The courtroom is filled up again in no time with animals of all shapes and sizes.

Even the wooden beams are packed full with flying and gliding creatures with a bat and an owl especially going at it with an argument about who deserved the tight spot they shared best.

Truly, the High Court of Dungalo has never seen an audience of this magnitude. It takes a while, after being settled, for the animals admitted into the courtroom to notice something peculiar.

King Migag II isn't present, and the court proceedings will soon begin.

This somewhat confirms the rumour that has been flying around since the day after King Migag II was handed the legal scroll at the carnival. Rumours claim that the King has fallen deathly ill from the shock of this case.

Prince Edgar, however, is seated at the defendant's bench with the Royal legal defence team. His posture is tense, but his chin is raised in a natural confidence peculiar to Lions. Some of the animals, especially the female ones, can be seen stealing sneaky glances at him, captivated by his charismatic aura.

Queen Sheila is noticeably absent, and a new rumour has it that she is the primary carer for her husband, the King, in his sick den.

It doesn't take long after for the Giraffe Judge, Judge Mavis, to stride in from her inner chambers, a smug air about her as she settles in her chair.

The Rhinoceros Bailiff straightens and begins.

"All rise! The High Court of Dungalo is now in session, with the Honourable Judge Mavis presiding."

Every animal stands, and some that have never attended a court case have to be first prompted by their more experienced neighbour before they can catch on. A mole nearly topples over his chair trying to keep up.

Judge Mavis peers at everyone through her low-sitting spectacles for a good moment before sniffing and turning her attention back to the files before her.

"You may be seated."

The court clerk, a spotted brown and white Cow, sets the floor. "Case Number 341. The Crown vs. The Citizens of Dungalo. Plaintiffs are a collective of concerned species represented today by Prosecutor Barr. Jones."

"Ah ah, before we proceed." Judge Mavis says', her lips turned down at the sides. "Can the skunks on the fourth row please be escorted out? I wouldn't want any unfortunate incidents like the last time."

The animals start murmuring as two security guards approach the now-terrified skunk and his young son to lead them outside.

"How unfair. It's not their fault they're created to be so… gassy." A goat bleats, and Judge Mavis' beady glare zeroes in on her.

"The she-goat may be escorted out as well for disrupting a court in session," she says, then stares around the courtroom with a challenge in her eyes. "And anyone else who has something to say, out of turn. Thank you."

The courtroom is quiet as the shocked she-goat scoffs indignantly and leaves on her own, muttering several things under her breath.

"There we go." Judge Mavis smiles, saccharine-like. "The prosecutor may now present their case."

Barr. Jones stands, looking as sophisticated as ever as he steps up to the front of the courtroom, brushing his already polished fur.

"Thank you, my Lord." He tips his head slightly, then continues. "my Lord, fellow citizens, we are gathered here to address the growing concerns about King Migag II's ability to rule Dungalo.

"In the past month, he's appointed a species with no formal history in combat or enforcement to serve as protectors. This, against enemy kingdoms with a stronger force and the common human enemy. What sort of decision-making is this?"

Jones continues, theatrically pulling a scroll from his case. "We submit that the appointment of the meerkats as Dungalo's security was reckless, dangerous, and purely symbolic. Since their appointment, crimes have not decreased, trust in the system has plummeted, and worst of all, our King has placed emotion over reason."

When Barr Jones is done speaking, he glances

toward the Tigers. Meevo catches his eyes and gives a pleased flick of his tail.

The courtroom breaks out into murmurs but is immediately silenced with one sweeping look from Judge Mavis.

She clears her throat and adjusts her spectacles. "Defence?"

Alia, a lioness from the royal legal defence team, steps up to the front of the courtroom and gives Judge Mavis a little head bow. She paces slowly, the faint click of her claws on the stone floor echoing as she speaks.

"The prosecution would have you believe that change equates to collapse. But what has truly collapsed? The security? Or the egos of those who no longer benefit from an outdated system?"

She subtly shoots a glance at the tigers, but they notice and growl lowly and Barr.

Jones tries to calm them down.

"The meerkats were elected by this very community. Their work has barely begun. How can they be judged before they've even been given a chance to implement their strategy?

"The decision to appoint the meerkats was made with the future in mind," Barr. Alia adds. "Not to cater to the powerful, but to protect the vulnerable. Is that not what true leadership is?"

Judge Mavis looks over her glasses. "Do you have tangible defence against the charges of negligence and disruption of order?"

"We do." Barr. Alia nods. "In the few weeks since the meerkats' appointment, we've seen more citizen involvement, higher community trust from smaller species, and not a single major threat to Dungalo's security. Crime has not increased. The only rise has been in whispers of discontent. Spread, I suspect, by those who fear losing control."

Gasps and nods ripple across the courtroom

"Objection, my Lord!" Barrr. Jones says heatedly. "The defendant is making very bold claims!"

Judge Mavis lifts a brow slowly. "And… your objection is?" "Speculative!" Barr. Jones fires back, a bit too quickly.

Judge Mavis sniffs. "Overruled. Continue, Barrister Alia. But mind the theatrics."

Barr. Alia nods gratefully and continues. "My Lord, the defence is ready to present witness statements that will reflect the true state of Dungalo under the meerkats' watch."

The courtroom murmurs.

Commander Jay and other meerkats

representatives who have been overcome with nerves this whole time exchange anxious glances. One of them starts wringing her tail as stress relief.

Alia gestures to the bailiff. "First witness, please." First to the stand is Greta, the elderly Goat librarian.

She testifies that since the meerkats took charge, she feels safer walking home at dusk after closing up the library. She also recounts an instance where a stolen figurine was retrieved by some meerkats who had witnessed the theft.

"I didn't file a report. They were there, they observed, and they acted."

Up next, a Rabbit vendor that looks like he will flee at the slightest noise comes up.

When he speaks, there's a slight stutter.

He recalls the meerkats de-escalating a fight that broke out in front of his market stall.

"J-Just with their w-words. They sure do h-have a way with w-words." Then comes Kellie, a young, adorable Squirrel and her mum.

According to Kellie's mum, during the carnival, Kellie had gotten lost, and she had panicked. However, she came across a meerkat that led her to a tent they set up to watch over lost children or items.

"The fact that they had thought of this and prepared for it was very thoughtful," Kellie's mum says. "When I got there, I saw my baby, safe and sound."

Kellie clings to her mum as she speaks next. "A kind meerkat stayed with me the whole time until my mum found me. He made shadow puppets too. I liked him."

The crowd reacts softly to this, and even Judge Mavis can't keep the smile off her face.

The meerkats in the gallery begin to loosen, and one even wipes a tear of joy.

Commander Jay lets out a breath that feels like it's been held since the beginning of this trial.

Things are going so well.

For the last witness, a large Owl night cleaner swoops down from the ceiling beams and onto the witness box, startling quite a number of people.

He confirms there's been "less madness" on his night shifts since the meerkats took over. "They're always present, without making a show of it. Their patrols do make me

feel much safer than before they were here."

Back at the defence table, Barr. Alia paces

slowly.

"These are only a few curated witness testimonies, my lord." She stops pacing and faces the spectators. "Many may not agree with our King's trust in the meerkats, but people are starting to see for themselves why the meerkats were always the right choice, just as King Migag II had seen for himself."

Barr. Alia turns to Judge Mavis, a little smile on her face. "We rest our case." Judge Mavis taps her gavel once. "Barr. Jones, rebuttal?"

He walks slowly to the centre of the floor, lips pursed.

"Emotional testimonies. Heartwarming stories. But none of this proves the meerkats are capable of managing a national crisis. Yes, they've kept things tidy for a few weeks. But should a major threat arise—"

The courtroom doors swing open.

Every head turns.

Two royal guards enter, and behind them is a figure so weak and pale yet upright. King Migag II is here.

Prince Edgar jolts up, rushing to his father, but King Migag II raises a paw slightly to stop him. "I am fine, son."

Gasps echo around the courtroom as the

animals notice the frail state of their king that had always been the epitome of strength and health.

Judge Mavis blinks, visibly shaken. "Your Majesty —"

"I will be brief," King Migag II says, voice coarse but strong. "I was advised not to come. My queen insisted I rest. But how can a king lie down when his people are being told he has failed them?"

He steps forward.

"I am not a perfect king. But I have never ruled with anything less than love. The decision to appoint the meerkats was not made on a whim. It was a response to the future I wish for all animals. One not ruled by fear or brute force, but by empathy."

He looks around the room.

"Some animals fear this change. But let them fear. Let them resist if they must. We will not return to an age of dominance and intimidation simply because progress makes some uncomfortable."

He turns to Judge Mavis, "I trust in this court. I trust in Dungalo. I trust the hearts of those that want the good and progress of Dungalo. And of course, I fully trust in the meerkats."

There is silence, only broken by Kellie's ill-timed cough and then a clap. Two claps.

Three. Until the whole courtroom is clapping in thunderous applause.

Even Judge Mavis is clapping until she remembers she has to be the impartial one.

So she quickly stops and clears her throat awkwardly as the applause dies down. "Ahem. Well then. Unless Barr. Jones has anything else to add—"

"No further remarks, my Lord." Barr. Jones says, although seething beneath the surface. Ever since becoming a lawyer, he had never known defeat. But here, in this courtroom, he knows a losing game when he sees one.

Scratch that. An already lost game.

Judge Mavis nods, adjusting her spectacles. "In that case, this court rules in favour of the Crown. The charges are dismissed."

The gavel drops and the defendants and their allies collectively let out a sigh of relief.

The nightmare is over.

Chapter Nine

The reigning peace in Dungalo can be said to have never been witnessed before.

After the city-state of Dungalo was created, things did get much better than they used to be. However, before the meerkats' appointment as the new security force, there were still petty- to medium-scale crimes. And on occasions, some large-scale crimes like targeted assaults were recorded, with perpetrators roaming free because they couldn't be traced.

In this new age of Dungalo, the security measures make it near impossible to get away with a crime of any scale. With the cutting-edge technology made for the meerkats in collaboration with the Tech Research department, every criminal is sure to be brought to book before they are even done committing their crime.

The precautionary measures definitely have

a hand in discouraging thoughts of crime among criminals, because there is a 98.2% chance of getting caught—according to a technology and social analyst, Von Pablo, the grey wolf.

However, there is something that social commentators have observed has a bigger hand in curbing and reducing the crime rates.

Unity.

The meerkats being elected to a top position from the unspoken societal bottom turned out to be a factor that promoted the peace of Dungalo. Many little critters allowed themselves to be inspired and went for roles they previously would never have gone for before—not because they are unqualified, but because there seemed to be an unspoken rule that a little critter should keep their dreams small.

With a surge of bold, little critters applying for big roles, there also came the realisation of just how valuable they were—especially for critical thinking skills and innovative ideas.

The respect that came from that was natural, and thus, the societal ranking system somewhat faltered, but in a good way. The animals started learning to see the other

animal as more than their societal ranking and for more of the value they brought.

This fostered a healthy, peaceful relationship

amongst the animals, and in a society with a healthy relationship, the members tend to look out for themselves a bit more.

It's also this unity and zero hesitance to look out for the other animal that allows for the meerkats to enlist the services of other creatures in security.

For example, the owls are engaged to help keep watch at night, due to their spectacular night sight, and the Eagles offer their long-distance eyesight for the position of aerial scouts.

The soldier ants are also included, housed strategically across Dungalo and the outskirts and all back to the meerkats' security barracks, in a way that would allow information to be seamlessly relayed in a couple of minutes.

There are also the chameleons, who are very valuable in stealth missions.

Most of the animals all have official roles to play, and this makes each and every one of them feel valued and important. Also, realising that the meerkats have no interest in monopolising power helped build the trust and respect that the animals quickly grew for them.

Indeed, the animals have not ever witnessed the reigning peace they experience today. However, the same cannot be said for outside the fortress walls of Dungalo.

For a long time, even before the reign of King Migag II, Yakko Forest has been dragging the borders with a neighbouring kingdom. Both parties claim that the other kingdom is trying to encroach on their lands, and no solid agreement has been reached.

King Migag II had managed to curb the conflict a little after being crowned, deciding to forfeit some of the Dungalo land for peace. And all was well for a while, until the other kingdom started trying to claim more land.

Everyone immediately understood what was happening.

The other kingdom viewed King Migag II as someone who would choose peace every time and thus give up everything required to have that peace. However, this time, King Migag II didn't budge and has been maintaining his stance since then.

That is, until his health started failing—significantly after the lawsuit against him.

And now, without the constant presence of the King, the neighbouring kingdom is getting bolder and bolder, deliberately setting up permanent sites far beyond the land that has been given to them.

This is the meerkats' current concern.

Even before being officially recognised as the

new security force when the crown won the case against the big cats, the meerkats had already begun an undercover project by sending a few agents — at different times — to dwell in the enemy Kingdom.

It took quite some time and a lot of cover stories, but the agents settled in nicely and didn't look a bit out of place.

They were scattered all over the enemy kingdom, leading very different lives, but two meerkats ended up working in the same pub. And it was here they discovered something that would dangerously topple the peace of Dungalo, enough to bring war.

*   *   *

The Chipped Talon is a pub owned by a large, bald Eagle named Heo. He'd inherited it from his father, who'd inherited it from his father, and it went on back like this for at least three more generations.

Heo takes a lot of pride in the family business and, thus, is very particular about the potential staff he hires. In fact, there are very particular rules that have made animals accuse him of being a thickheaded bigot, but in order to keep up the legacy and performance of The Chipped Talon, Heo stands by them.

For example, the skunks are welcome to the pub only if they accept the outdoor area reserved for them. Skunks are never hired as staff; however, many have tried and failed.

Another one of these rules had banned Ospreys from being either staff or customers because of a long-standing, inherited beef between the Eagles and the Ospreys. To be fair, an Osprey family had their own business that they banned all Eagles from, as well.

These are only a couple of Heo's rules and he strictly abides by them. However, even when not fitting into any of his ban lists as a potential staff member, even the hiring process is usually rough, as Heo runs thorough background checks on every applicant.

The story of how an undercover meerkat— Elaine–from Dungalo makes it is one for another day, but it seems her cover story managed to be convincing enough to get the job she's been at for years now.

The pub is a good place to get valuable information, after sifting away all the drunken rants or fluffed-up rumours. If you listen closely enough, you can get something good enough.

This is how Elaine found out about the plans to sabotage specific merchant caravans from Dungalo. The information had been relayed, and the merchants' paths had been rerouted while willing, trained aides took the ambush path.

That had given Dungalo the upper hand in catching the enemy kingdom's cruelty red-handed, since they usually denied using underhand means even when evidence is stacked on them.

That had been Elaine's first major breakthrough.

However, tonight, she might have found much larger news than a caravan ambush.

The pub is packed tonight, as it always is because *The Chipped Talon* has been an animal favourite for literal generations.

Elaine is having an especially difficult time at the bar because just that morning, Heo had fired the second staff member that worked with her for consistently getting orders wrong.

For the sake of the mission, and with how easy it is for Heo to fire his staff with no prior notice, Elaine never formed deeper relationships with the other staff of *The Chipped Talon*. But her coworker's absence is affecting her now, though, because they'd figured out a teamwork that makes dealing with the crowded pub easier. Now, Elaine has to handle all that herself.

It is during this struggle to handle several impatient orders at once that Elaine notices two hooded figures trying to blend into the crowded pub. They look a lot like Lions which, at first sight, don't seem out of place; the lions of the enemy kingdom aren't as careful or particular about their image as the lions of Dungalo.

What sells them out, however, is their scents, for you see, meerkats have a very strong sense of smell and retentive olfactory memory. Elaine can tell who is a repeating customer and a first-time customer just from their scents alone.

And these scents tell her that these two are here for the first time. The first belongs to an unfamiliar lioness; however, the second is the one that stumps her. For it's been a while since she's come across that scent.

A long time ago, in Dungalo.

It's Prince Edgar, son of King Migag II.

What he is doing in the enemy kingdom that has been cruel to Dungalo on several occasions is unclear, but Elaine is determined to find out.

Luckily, Prince Edgar and the other lionesses are there for the whole of Elaine's remaining shift, talking to different animals. At that moment, Elaine starts to desperately wish that she was a waitress – which was initially her intended position; however, Heo deemed her diligent enough to teach how to mix drinks at the bar.

The two leave five minutes before Elaine's shift ends, and she is almost tempted to follow along, but she can't blow her cover yet and have Heo fire her. So she bears it out until the very minute she clocks out.

One good thing about working with Heo is that he never keeps his staff past the time they're supposed to clock out, not even for a favour, and Elaine is out of there as soon as she's done.

She can still smell Prince Edgar and the other lioness, so she tracks them, making sure to stay out of the wind direction that could expose her position to them. Eventually, she catches up, seeing the two hooded figures leisurely walking together in the distance.

Stealthily, Elaine catches up in the shadows, close enough to hear them.

"—make sure my father doesn't find out." Elaine hears the lioness finding out. "Not now; we're so close."

"You don't have to tell me," Prince Edgar chuckles. "I wouldn't want to get on the wrong side of the King before I get the chance to ask for his daughter's hand."

The other lioness giggles and slightly bumps into him. "If all fails, we can always elope."

"Anything for you, my love." Prince Edgar brushes against her. "But we have to first complete our mission."

The Princess of the Enemy Kingdom straightens. "Of course. I never forgot about that."

Elaine follows for a few more minutes but soon falls back to not push her luck in not being caught. She's in shock but holds it together as she sprints to the outskirts of the enemy kingdom to relay a message to the ants that have been positioned there.

The head of the chain crawls out of the ground hole when Elaine puts a drop of nectar beside it; a code.

"Tell the commander that this is a code red," Elaine says, urgently. "The Prince of Dungalo is in relations with the Princess of the Enemy Kingdom. Their plans are yet unknown, so we must proceed with caution."

The soldier ant salutes, then crawls back into the ground hole to begin the chain.

As Elaine heads back to her little abode, she can't help shake the feeling that something is about to go very wrong. Very wrong, indeed.

And her intuition is right, for that night, when the message is relayed to Commander Jay, it is overheard by the wrong animal. One that has been lying in wait for years, to get a chance to topple Dungalo for good.

Chapter Ten

The Royal Chambers are designed to provide optimum comfort to all who reside in it.

It's spacious, well-ventilated and equipped with the best furniture to make the space feel like a haven you can rest in after a long day.

However, no matter the luxury that the royal chambers offer, it's not enough to improve the health of the dying King of Dungalo.

Queen Sheila is present in the room as the Royal Physician attends to King Migag II this evening, as she always is. Mostly because she likes to see what the physician is doing so she can try and administer the same care to the King to the best of her ability.

Although the treatment isn't much—just

some acupuncture point massage and administering a calming draught every eight hours.

In the years King Migag II has been ill, several physicians from far and near have been consulted, yet not one could nurse the King back to perfect health. One had mentioned the illness being something to do with the state of the mind manifesting on the body and advised everyone around the King to make sure they don't add to the strain.

The physician also recommended daily walks, which King Migag II did until his body could no longer. And so now, he's on a constant stream of calming draughts and massage as an effort to relax him and maybe distract him from his mind.

Nothing has been working, however, and each passing day, the King's health worsened.

"As always, my Queen, please remember to administer the medicine every 8 hours." The Royal Physician says, handing the Queen a new tonic. "God bless the King and may he get better."

Queen Sheila takes the little bottle from the physician and clutches it tightly. "Thank you."

"Does my queen require my services further?" "You may go."

The physician bows and holds the position for a few seconds before straightening and leaving.

Queen Sheila solemnly stays by her husband's side for a few more minutes before stepping out of his chambers.

Without the King around, most of the decision-making regarding the Kingdom has been left to her, and sometimes Prince Edgar.

In the early days of King Migag II's illness, she had frequently consulted him regarding these matters, but after the physician asked them not to add to his mental stress, she stopped.

Still, Queen Sheila refuses to let anyone outside the palace know how bad the King's health has become, even if she knows rumours have started spreading. She would keep the true details to herself because a confirmation of the rumours is more damning than the speculations.

She decides to take a short walk through the west gardens, her mind heavy with matters she doesn't want to think about, but when she walks a distance, she notices a commotion at a far archway.

Two of the gorilla guards stand firm, blocking the way of a tall, hunched figure as dark as night.

A royalist. And she knows of this one:

Jerome, the pack leader.

Even from this distance, she feels the small shift of the air that always comes when a Royalist is near, as if their presence alone carried a sinister aura with it.

She moves closer, catching fragments of the guards' firm refusals.

"You're not on the visitor's list. You can leave your message at the gates."

Jerome's voice carries a smooth sharpness. "The message is not for scribes; it is for the Queen's ears only. Tell her it concerns the future of Dungalo..." Jerome looks up and catches her eyes. "...and the prince."

The Queen stops a few paces away.

She could easily let the guards send him away, knowing that the Royalists have no interest but their own selfish ones. For all she knew, this could be a ploy to cause chaos.

However, she knows her husband would have given even those he disagreed with a chance.

He had tried, early in his reign, to give the Royalists another chance, offering them positions in the civic council where they could advise on heritage matters, which is definitely an honour to most, but to the Royalists, an insult.

They were too proud to serve in what they viewed as an inferior government, and so they had left Yakko Forest for the far outskirts, where they could keep their own company and their own rules.

Queen Sheila would rather not grant a Royalist an audience but King Migag II would and might even offer them tea because he was – is – a King that believes in giving everyone a chance, no matter their history.

Sighing, Queen Sheila signals for the guards to let him through.

The gorillas exchange a glance but eventually uncross their spears to let Jerome through. The latter is smug and gives them a dirty look before sauntering into the palace grounds to meet the waiting queen.

He bows a few feet away from her, only slightly but enough to not be accused of disrespect. "My Queen."

Queen Sheila keeps her voice levelled. "You consider whatever this is as urgent, I take it?"

"I'm afraid so, my Queen." Jerome says, keeping his voice low and conspiratorial. "There have been whispers from the wrong mouths about the prince on enemy soil, mingling with dangerous company."

"Dangerous company." Queen Sheila

deadpans.

"Prince Edgar has been seen associating with the princess of the enemy kingdom." Jerome says, eyes narrow. "In the wrong hands, this information can be a lethal blow."

"And how, Jerome, did *you* come across this information?" She can't help the sting in her voice. "And why are you graciously sharing it with me when you can be the wrong hand handling this information? I know Royalists have no cares but for themselves."

His beak twitches, but he doesn't break eye contact.

"You get it wrong, my Queen. We do care for Dungalo." he says, but not convincingly enough as he brushes against a dahlia flower the same shade as his feathers. "As do the meerkats, who know of this information and can use it to bring the downfall of the Royal Bloodline."

Queen Sheila locks her jaw. "The meerkats have served faithfully. They will at least inform me if —"

Jerome tilts his head. "Faithful to whom? To the crown, or to their own sense of justice? If they declare the Prince a threat to Dungalo, it will not matter what his true intentions are. The court of public opinion will not hesitate. Do you truly think they will shield him if it comes to their so-called 'duty'?"

Queen Sheila wants to retaliate, but she can't find the words as the question settles in her mind. When it comes down to it... Are the meerkats loyal to the kingdom or to the crown?

"You speak as though they would deliberately try to harm us," she retorts weakly. "I speak as one who has seen how easily a celebrated one can let duty blind them

to compassion... like the Royalists, maybe?" Jerome tuts, then laughs at the Queen's unimpressed expression. "The meerkats have grown popular—too popular, and that popularity is a weapon. If the people believe them, you could lose the Prince—and the entire royal bloodline—before you ever have a chance to defend yourselves."

The Queen swallows hard. It is not that she trusts Jerome. She doesn't. But the thought of Edgar's name dragged through the mud, branded as a traitor before he can even speak for himself, makes her stomach knot.

"The Royalists do nothing without some benefit; you are right about that," Jerome admits, plucking a black dahlia. "Which is why I'm here. Our glory days may be over, but we're still relatively at peace because we have a king who never encouraged the public to lynch us."

Queen Sheila stares hard at him without comment.

Jerome continues. "I'm sure you know that many eye the throne, but only one will be brave enough to take it."

"What do you mean?"

"When the reign of the lions falls, who do you think would take over and still be celebrated for it?" Jerome doesn't wait for an answer. "The tigers. This is why they led that lawsuit against the King, and from the number of signatures they got, we now know that some would always keep wishing that the tigers ruled instead."

"That's nonsense."

"Like you said, we are selfish. If I truly didn't have fear of the tigers taking the crown, do you think I'd be here warning you of it?" Jerome says. "I might not be in support of this current reign of lions, but I'd take it anytime over the tigers."

He drops the dahlia on the ground before the queen. "That is all I came to say. Ask your son where he's been when he returns."

Long after Jerome leaves, Queen Sheila is still unsettled.

She is aware of her son being away on

"diplomatic matters", but with the responsibility of looking after King Migag II, she lost track of time and is now realising that Edgar has been away for over a month.

She rushes to her chamber and sifts through the letters she's gotten but not opened in the past month and finds one from Edgar sent just a couple of days ago. Apparently, he's trying to settle a trading dispute, among other responsibilities.

And coincidentally, he sets his return date today by dusk. So she waits.

The sun had nearly dipped when he finally arrived, brushing dust from his mane as though it were a normal day. Queen Sheila wastes no time. "Where have you been this past month?"

He glances up sharply, then recovers. "Negotiating a trade concession. Several shipments were at risk."

Her stare doesn't shift. "And the Princess of the Enemy Kingdom was involved in this trade?"

For a second, something unreadable flickers in his eyes. "We crossed paths." "Crossed paths?" Her voice hardens. "I know you've been with her."

His composure falters. "Mother, I..."

"Don't lie to me, Edgar. You were seen with her."

He sighs but keeps his tone firm. "It's true, I have—"

"Gods, Edgar!" Queen Sheila exclaims and starts pacing around exasperatedly. "But it's not what it seems like, Mother."

"Then what is it?" she asks, stopping sharply in front of him He hesitates, then exhales. "We… are in a relationship…"

Queen Sheila closes her eyes like she feels a headache coming. "Oh, gods." "But it's not sinister, and that's not all to it." Prince Edgar quickly adds. "We are

trying to bring peace between our Kingdoms, to finally—"

She moves closer, whispering sharply. "Do you understand what this could cost you? Cost us? Regardless of your aim? If the wrong animals learn of this, they will not wait for explanations. They will call you a traitor, Edgar. They will demand punishment."

"I will explain," Edgar says desperately as his mother shakes her head in denial. "I-I can handle it."

"You cannot." Her voice shakes now. "Your enemies will use this to destroy you. And if the meerkats —"

"The meerkats would never make me a target, Mother."

"But they will do their duty above all else," she snaps. "And duty will not protect you from their findings."

"Mother, I–"

"Now you will listen to me carefully, Edgar", she says, the edge of command creeping in. "And you will end this. You will never see her again." He opens his mouth to protest, but she cuts him off. "This is not a request. If you care for this kingdom and for your future, you will obey."

The conversation leaves her trembling. By the time she leaves his chambers, her decision is already forming, fuelled by Jerome's words and her own fear.

The meerkats must be stopped before they get the chance to ruin her family and their reputation.

But first, she must ask for forgiveness.

Because without the power of the King, she isn't sure she can successfully pull off what she's about to do next.

God bless the King, but she's about to do something wicked.

Chapter Eleven

"The meerkats have been declared enemies of the city-state of Dungalo on command of King Migag II. If you see one, immediately alert a royal guard or the new elite security force of Cheetahs near you. The meerkats have been seen mingling with enemies on enemy soil and are not to be trusted. Be warned; anyone seen associating with a meerkat will also be found guilty of treason. God bless the King and his determination to protect us all."

"Turn that down; I hear something." Commander Jay says to a teen aged meerkat holding the only radio they have.

The young meerkat immediately turns the broadcast radio down to zero, and every other meerkat in the underground space falls silent, ears perked up.

There indeed is rustling above them, and Commander Jay silently motions for some of his remaining officers to form a protective rank in case anything goes wrong. In the months that the meerkats have been living here, they have created a fully functioning underground hideout bunker with several escape tunnels that lead to safety.

When they were suddenly declared enemies of the state, there had been no chance for a lot of meerkats. The moment the announcement aired live, the homes and security barracks were invaded by the Cheetahs and other supporting big cats.

Lots of meerkats were captured that day, and a lot of meerkat families were separated brutally. The handful that were lucky enough to escape ended up being scattered all over Dungalo, as the gates and borders were heavily guarded.

Some stayed in hiding only briefly before being discovered and arrested to join the rest in the forgotten dungeons that King Migag had previously shut down.

However, some other meerkats-in-hiding were discovered first by Commander Jay who had set up a team to drill underground tunnels in discreet locations that could connect them to beyond Dungalo.

These tunnels lead to different underground bases that ensure that even if a base is found, other meerkats can still have a chance to escape.

Every other day, ex meerkat officers would risk their lives to go search for other meerkats-in-hiding or get a scope of what was happening in Dungalo. Sometimes they came back with outside news and more terrified but grateful meerkats; other times some ex officers never came back at all.

A recent expedition had brought back the radio that they are currently using to tune in to Dungalo news, with the broadcast about the meerkats being played twice a day every single day.

None of the meerkats have yet to grasp why this sudden witch-hunt is targetted at them. The highranking officers, however, know that King Migag II had no hand in this for they are aware of the King's actual condition but have kept it secret from the public at the request of the Queen.

This information, however, is shared to every meerkat they rescue from within Dungalo, to dissuade them from fixating on a redherring used to distract them from what might actually be happening.

The rustling above gets closer, circling around the hidden entrance. Eventually, there's a rhythmic tapping on the contraption skillfully covering the entrance and Commander Jay and the rest of the meerkats relax. It's a secret knock.

"Open it." he orders and two meerkats get to work with unlatching the locks and subtly pushing the door up.

"It's lieutenant Jeremy back with a meerkat child." one of the officers on watch duty above ground informs. He, and other officers on above ground duty, are also responsible for sweeping the leaves back on the door.

The meerkat child is lowered first and then Lieutenant Jeremy follows suit, having the door shut above him.

"I found him in a dumpster behind Lily, the old Chimp's house." Lieutenant Jeremy informs after saluting. "Apparently, she's been sheltering him but had asked him to hide in there when the impromptu house checks started."

The meerkat child in question is shaking like a leaf and looking like he's shed more than a few tears. A female meerkat swoops in to wrap her arms around him.

"This is Helen's son," she informs, shaking her head in a form of a secret message.

A parent of his was taken. "But his father is in the western bunker, I believe. We were rescued together."

The meerkat child's eyes light up at the detail of his father being free.

"Can I see my daddy?" he asks, and the female meerkat smiles down gently at him with a nod before looking up at the officers.

Commander Jay clears his throat. "We'll make arrangements to transfer him to the western bunker, but for now he has to be taken care of."

Other meerkats swoop into action to prepare a bath, some food and a bed for the meerkat child as Commander Jay turns back to his lieutenant.

"We still have some support then?"

Lieutenant Jeremy nods. "It seems. What old Lily did is dangerous—the royalists don't care if it's a child or an aged animal, association with the meerkats gets them in the Dungeon."

"Bless her. She always used to bake the best bread to share with locals."

"As selfless as Al, her husband." Lt Jeremy acknowledges and then straightens. "I heard disturbing news while out in the city."

"What kind of news?"

"I hear the Queen is about to sign a peace treaty…" Lt Jeremy drops his voice. "...with the human race."

Commander Jay is solemn. "Are the rumours of the Queen losing her mind perhaps true?"

"Working with royalists tends to have that effect," Lt Jeremy says. "Masterminds at manipulation and slowly breaking the mind from within."

Commander Jay sighs and rubs a paw on his face aggressively. "I need to visit one of the eastern bunkers and see how the training is going."

"There's been progress," Lt Jeremy confirms. "I heard a young meerkat maintained his position on two legs for about 3 minutes."

Commander Jay rubs another aggressive paw over his face. That isn't enough. The meerkats have to learn to stand on their two feet for longer than 30 minutes at least.

With no animal aid or high watchtowers to help them keep watch, they all have to make up for it with the height from standing on their rear legs.

Might not be enough, but keeping watch to alert others for unwelcome intrusion is all they can do now and they have to do it well.

The future of the meerkats is currently uncertain, so they must protect the present they have now.

No matter what it takes.

*   *   *

A day after the peace treaty with the human race is signed, the Queen addresses the public on the claim that it is on behalf of her husband King Migag II.

She claims that this is to foster a better relationship where animals don't have to live in fear anymore.

"The humans will provide us with resources needed to scale our city-state of Dungalo to greater heights and to fight the enemy Kingdom that has been hurting us for too long," she says on the broadcast radio as every animal cowers in their abode in fear. "This is atonement for all the years of suffering they had put us through, so do not fret.

All is well."

Whispers of "the Queen has gone mad" started circulating the moment the Royalists were reinstated as Royal Advisors because most animals knew, even without confirmation, that King Migag II had no hand in this madness happening.

Now, there have been more rumours about the Queen's madness that seem to have solid footing.

"She just mutters away to herself, but no thought seems to be behind those eyes," a Pelican that worked in the royal palace confides in a friend at a bar. "Once I came across her staring at a tree, unmoving. Went in the palace to complete my tasks that took over an hour. Came back to see her still standing there."

Her friend, a swan, looks about before leaning in, whispering. "It must be the work of the royalists. They are said to have a dark magic that corrupts the mind of anyone that lets their words settle in their mind."

A look of realisation crosses the Pelican's face. "What if all this while, the past Kings of the dark era were controlled by the royalists, and we all thought it was the other way round?"

"My grandfather says it's an open secret that the older generations knew," the swan says in a conspiratorial tone. "This is why they all feared the royalists more than they feared the Kings. Everyone knew they were the ones with the true power."

"But what do they gain from all the wickedness?" the Pelican asks, genuinely confused.

"Power is poison in the minds of... weak things," she says. "It corrupts and makes you want more. But when you always want more, there's nothing to gain. And that creates a void where you're never satisfied."

"Hm. "Philosophical," the Pelican says as

she sips on her drink that has gotten warm, not noticing the cloaked figure seated close to them and staring into its drink.

Before dusk arrived that day, the pelican, the swan and her grandfather went missing.

When dawn arrives the next day, news that plunges the animals into further despair is broadcast.

The great King that brought peace and progress after nearly a century of terror, King Migag II, has passed away.

Chapter Twelve

*P*rince Edgar has finally found it.

The one thing that can bridge the gap between the two kingdoms that were once one decades ago. And it's what he least expected.

Sniffing the air, he catches a whiff of a familiar smell nearby and he immediately whips his head to face Commander Jay.

"Your Highness." The meerkat bows, a funny sight because he's actually standing on two legs; a funny sight to behold. "How did you find our base?"

Prince Edgar smiles. "I can be a good tracker if I am keen on it. Although I suspect you wanted to be found by me instead."

Commander Jay smiles, tipping his head in respect. "By the two of you, you mean?"

There is some rustling in a bush nearby, and

out comes the Princess of the… other kingdom. For the meerkats have now realised who the real enemy is, and it is not the Kingdom that was once one with them.

"I just didn't want to scare anyone off with my presence. I mean no harm," she says as she approaches. "Princess Elena at your service."

Commander Jay bows once more. "I am deeply honoured."

"Shall we get to it?" Prince Edgar asks, and Commander Jay nods.

"I would invite you inside but our shelter is currently not big enough for the both of you," he jokes. "There's a safer place to discuss it, however."

He leads them to a thick canopy of trees that is flanked by several meerkat guards keeping an eye out for intruders or hidden eavesdroppers.

"We have learnt our lesson from last time," Commander Jay says. "We deduced that we were overheard discussing our… findings, and that was used to convince the Queen of apparently plotting treason."

Princess Elena bows her head in regret.

"I apologise that it came to this. We do, but Edgar has told me about your clan and how well you served Dungalo. I don't believe you were planning to harm us, at least not without confirming what is happening."

"We have no grudges against anyone but the ones who are abusing their power."

Prince Edgar straightens. "I also apologise for everything turning out like this but my father has no hand in this. And my mother may have done this but I assure you that she is not herself anymore."

"Not herself?" Commander Jay enquires curiously.

"She's slowly losing her own agency." Prince Edgar says. "When I speak to her, her eyes are blank and it feels like my mother is gone, and there's just her shell left."

His voice lowers to a whisper at the last words and Princess Elena places a comforting paw on his.

"We'll get her back." she whispers and Prince Edgar gives a small smile before turning back up towards Commander Jay.

"That's why we're here, to come together and stop this madness." he says, determined. "To bring back the world my father envisioned and created."

Commander Jay is solemn as he asks. "But how do we do that? As far as we know, the human race is getting involved. Your father managed to cast them out somehow when he was crowned, so I'm sure this time they'll be prepared."

"And prepared they are." Princess Elena says as she brings out a scroll from her robes. "We were doing some snooping in the human race base and found something. I took a quick sketch because we didn't want to let them know we were there."

Commander Jay looks at her curiously as he takes it and rolls it open. "It's a battle plan."

"An incomplete one, but that's what we found." she says, sighing. "They have plans to wage war on my Kingdom, using the citizens of Dungalo."

"The animals of Dungalo may be frustrated by your Kingdom, but I don't think they'd willingly ever go to war over the borders. We value peace above all, given our history."

"We suspect the humans might be used as some form of "answer" to the border problem, where they offer Dungalo help to take back our land." Prince Edgar says.

Commander Jay sneaks a look at Princess Elena to know what she thinks of Prince Edgar claiming the borderland is for Dungalo.

She waves a paw. "It's obvious it's for

Dungalo. My father and the council can be greedy."

Commander Jay hides a smile. "But what are they gaining in return?"

"The crystals in the riverbeds stretching from Dungalo to my Kingdom." Princess Elena says. "We don't have much use for it, but for keeping our watering holes clean, but apparently it's a great treasure for them to power up their technology."

"At least, that's what I know the humans took during the evil reigns of my forefathers." Prince Edgar says. "There are notes on it in the Royal archives that I came across when I was a young lion."

The whole thing is still a bit overwhelming for Commander Jay to wrap his head around. He can't believe the royalists would be as selfish as giving away resources meant for the people in return for personal gains.

"So, what's the plan, your highnesses?" he asks. "What can we possibly do?" "Strategise for war and create alliances." Prince Edgar says. "Before I left Dungalo, I

overheard a ploy to exile the Tigers, possibly because the Royalists feel threatened by them. When that happens, we will seek them out to join our cause."

"The tigers can be difficult. That is a near impossible plan."

"You convinced my father of your plans to protect Dungalo, not because you are a sweet talker but because you thought out your ideas and truly believed in them." Prince Edgar smiles. "If you believe in the cause of taking back Dungalo from evil hands, I'm sure you can convince the tigers."

Commander Jay bows a little. "Thank you for your confidence in me, your highness. However, no matter how strong the tigers are, we are still outnumbered."

"Not to worry, we have secretly rallied up willing supporters in my Kingdom." Princess Elena says. "And Prince Edgar has been doing the same in Dungalo, way before this all started."

"You knew about the war?" Commander Jay asks, confused.

"We didn't. We were trying to settle the border dispute and bring about peaceful coexistence between our Kingdoms." Prince Edgar says. "The supporters are from the people who shared our views. However, the willing ones in Dungalo can't join us because the city borders are being watched."

"And he can't go back either to maybe inform them of us because I'm sure these royalists know he's up to something."

"Hm. If you have a list of names, the meerkats can pass on the information during our rescue runs inside Dungalo." Commander Jay offers to the interest of the two Royalty. He shakes his head. "I'm sorry, but I can't let you know about it. The mission is already fragile in itself."

"Yes, yes, I understand." Prince Edgar says and then procures several parchments from his robes. "I do have a list written in code, but I'll write a new one before we leave. Thank you."

As Prince Edgar gets to transcribing the codes with fresh parchment sheets that the meerkats have gotten, Commander Jay looks curiously between the two royals.

"Permit me to ask, your highness," he starts. "But how did you two meet?"

Princess Elena is suddenly flustered and Prince Edgar makes an unintended mark on his parchment, equally flustered.

"Eh, we crossed paths one day." Princess Elena says, too quickly. "Yes, yes, we did." Prince Edgar backs it up.

Seeing as they refuse to share any more detail apart from that, Commander Jay does not dare probe more.

He hides a secret smile because these two might not know it but with their relationship, they are already closer to the peace of the two Kingdoms than they know.

Chapter Thirteen

The funeral of King Migag II is a glum affair, and not just because the animals have lost the icon of peace and progress.

If it were normal times, the animals might have had a hand in organising the funeral; every animal would want to participate in that. There would be great mourning, but there would also be a celebration of King Migag II's life as a show of gratitude for how great of a King he was.

However, the animals had no such liberty to do this.

The funeral is fully organised by the royalist, taking control of every single thing from picking workers to put the event together down to a very specific programme of the event.

When the day finally comes, the animals show up, not only as respect to their King but also in fear of what would happen if they didn't.

The Queen, with Royal Guards carrying

King Migag II's casket, is flanked by Cheetahs and Royalists as she starts the procession through the Glebel until they are at the front stage, where King Migag's casket is laid down.

The whole ceremony is stifling, with the Royalists staring down as many animals as they could and the elite Cheetah security force parading past the animals every other minute, showing off the uniform gear developed by the tech research team that they've been adorned with.

The worst of it all is the Queen's vacant stare and actions, barely making any action of her own unless prompted by a Royalist. Prince Edgar himself isn't around. He hasn't been since the reign of the Royalists returned, and the animals are starting to feel the absence of genuine care for their wellbeing. There is not one figure of authority present in the hall that they feel like they could trust.

Finally, the whole dreary affair draws to an end, and a royalist prompts the Queen to give a speech.

"My beloved subjects," she begins, her words monotonous and devoid of inflections. "It is with a heavy heart that I address you in this time of sorrow. However, life, and the future of Dungalo, must continue. My husband, King Migag II–may he rest in peace–desired nothing more than everlasting safety and prosperity for all of us."

She pauses, seemingly waiting for a response that doesn't come. The crowd remains silent, a sea of worried and terrified faces. Jerome leans in, his beak brushing against her ear as he whispers something. This prompts her to continue, her voice gaining a forced, almost hypnotic cadence. "To honour his vision, and in light of the continuous threats from the enemy kingdom, I have, on behalf of the Crown, formally enacted the Peace Treaty with the human race."

None of the animals feel particularly at peace with this new development promised to bring them peace. But no one dares to speak... that is, until a Beaver loudly opposes.

"T-This doesn't make any sense!" she says, visibly shaking from fear or anger or both. The beady eyes of all the royalists zone in on her. "King Migag would never have wanted this! Dungalo was built to protect us from the human race, but the minute the King is gone, the doors are opened to the very enemy we shut out."

The voice of one is enough to encourage the voice of a hundred, and soon many join in to protest.

"That's right! We oppose this!" a black bear

shouts. "This is not the Dungalo we built!"

"We do not consent to this!"

And soon, the Glebel is filled with the voices of the animals who have been given freedom of speech and expression after years of tyranny and would not let it be taken away again.

However, the next moment is a blur of disaster.

From screaming out their dissatisfaction, animals soon find themselves inhaling a pungent, toxic cloud of smoke that is coming from several little tubes the elite force is throwing about.

Their eyes sting and their throats burn, and one of the last things some of them see is the Queen being safely led out of the Glebel, in a nose mask, through a door. In tow are the Royalists looking down at them with smug grins on their faces.

This is when the animals realise that it's too late. The freedom they're trying to fight for has already been taken from them.

And getting it back, if they're brave enough, is going to be a bloody affair.

*   *   *

Commander Jay is on a mission that he is

nearly sure will get him killed, but he has no other choice but to forge through. He creeps through the dingy forest on his two rear legs, clumsy but still more stable than most meerkats have been able to achieve.

With the revelation of potential war that Prince Edgar and Princess Elena had shown, the meerkats have been more intense with both their sentinel training and their offence and defence strategies.

And there have been improvements; the young meerkat that had held his standing stance for an hour is now able to hold it for over 6 hours before crumpling, and that is admirable because the whole exercise is excruciating for the meerkats.

They aren't born knowing how to stand, and so trying to deliberately gain the skill of standing and moving on their rear legs is damaging to their joints. But they have to go through this now so they can evolve and give future generations of meerkats an advantage.

They have also rescued some of the animals on Prince Edgar's list, as long as they could fit in through their tunnels. Animals like the Squirrels and Gerbils and Hedgehogs. They were distributed across the underground bunkers as well and have been actively contributing to war strategies and undergoing their own training.

However, for a few weeks now, rescue missions have not been carried out within Dungalo because the security has become stifling, and no rescue missions means no

intel either, especially since there has not been relevant news on the meerkat radio for a long time.

They suspect it's because the Royalists prefer to speak to the animals face-to-face to assert dominance or something.

However, before information went dark, the meerkats learnt about humans in the walls of Dungalo, putting strange contraptions on the animals. And once the contraptions have been put on, it's impossible for the average animal to take them off.

Luckily, there are some meerkats that used to be in the Tech Research team, and once a discarded tag was acquired by Prince Edgar and Princess Elena in a risky mission back to the human base, the meerkats started probing and analysing the human race's technology.

It turns out that it's a tracking tag that can also tune into the animals' live location and feed; see where they are; hear what they see; see what they see.

Luckily, there's a loop in this — they can't all be watched at the same time because their locations are only updated every seemingly random number of minutes — which the tech research team was able to figure out the sequence to.

The tech research assumes that the humans would only tune in live to animals they find moving suspiciously, and there should be a limit cap to how many animals can be live-tuned into at the same time. So going about their normal day should be fine.

Yet, it's still risky because no animal would know who the humans decide to tune into next, and if it would be done at an incriminating moment. And the meerkats are worried if the animals even know what the tag is and are careful with what they say or do.

Commander Jay finds it ironic how, in the beginning of their exile, the meerkats had focused on just rescuing the rest of them and staying low-key. However, they've now come to a point where they're back to picking back the duty they had.

The duty to protect.

And this is why Commander Jay is risking everything to make sure they have the upper hand in this whole fiasco.

Just one word: Tigers. They've been recently exiled from Dungalo, just like Prince Edgar and

Princess Elena had predicted. It seemed Royalists were working overtime to get rid of everyone they deemed problematic through the Queen.

It took a while, but the meerkats found out where the Tigers had set up a community for themselves, smack in the middle of Dungalo and the enemy Kingdom. But before they could reach out the first time, the Tiger clan was attacked by humans.

That was a few weeks ago, but their new community has been discovered again by scouting meerkats, and now, Commander Jay is going to try his luck with creating an alliance with the Tigers.

Commander Jay hears a snarl before being knocked down and feeling a suffocating weight pressed down on his upper body.

"Well, well, well, what do we have here?" Meevo breathes down on him, the snarl still on his face. "A meerkat."

"How dare an enemy of the Kingdom encroach on our territory?" another voice asks, and Mario emerges from the shadows. "The disrespect."

"Brothers, he must have a reason for being here." Raymond sighs as other tigers start emerging from the shadows.

"And how bold he must be when the

meerkats are the very reason we're in this mortifying situation." Meevo growls. "Brother, how can you want to reason with him?"

"Because great-grand-father would hear him out." Raymond says, and Meevo snorts mockingly.

"No, he wouldn't."

"He would, and we also should." Raymond says and looks to his elder brother for support.

Mario is silent for a moment before he sharply turns to Commander Jay. "Why are you here, little critter?"

Commander Jay makes a series of high wheezing noises as he tries to speak, and Meevo raises a brow at him. "Are you perhaps challenged in some way?"

Raymond sighs."You're crushing his windpipe, Meevo. Take your paw off him."

Meevo chuckles delightedly as he realises his brother is right but instantly removes his paw from the nearly strangulated Commander Jay.

He spits and sputters for a while before finding his voice, but when he speaks, there's still a bit of wheeze in his voice. He looks down at Mario's front leg, then back up at the tigers.

"I am here to help and ask for help in return."

The tigers are silent until Meevo breaks it. "Can I put my paw back on him? He's not making any sense."

"Be clear." Mario growls as Commander Jay jumps and takes several steps away from Meevo and his paw.

"I'll show you instead," he says as he takes out a tiny remote from a sling bag. All the tigers immediately go into high alert.

"What is that!?" Meevo snarls before pouncing on Commander Jay once more, but the remote button has already been pressed.

"Y-You're free." Commander Jay wheezes under the returned weight of Meevo's paw.

His eyes are on Mario's front leg and every eye narrows in on it. The tag that was previously wrapped around his front leg snugly has fallen off.

There is silence for a while before Mario speaks up, sounding humbled. "How did you do that? We've been trying all we can to get it off."

"This is how I can help you." Commander Jay says, pushing at Meevo's paw. The Tiger gets off him. "The meerkats have been watching, and we know about the human race attacking you and capturing some of your own. That tag led them to you."

"We know. Which is why we've been very alert to any being that steps into our territory after the last ambush." Mario snarls as he kicks the tag a long distance away. "I was cornered and drugged while on a walk, which is why they were able to get it on me in the first place."

"Now, what do you want?" Meevo asks, impatiently.

"Your alliances are all I ask." Commander Jay says. "We have a rebellion. Those who are willing to fight back for Dungalo. To get back the families they've lost, just as you have."

"And why do you think we'll want to join your little cause?" Mario asks in a tone that causes Commander Jay to break out in a cold sweat. "Last time we gave ears to a creature asking us to do the same, it ended in our shame and was the evidence that was used to exile us for treason."

Commander Jay blinks. "You weren't the ones behind the lawsuit?"

"We knew of the dark magic of the vultures, yet we let their words settle in our minds." Raymond says, sighing with disappointment. "I'm sure the Queen has fallen prey to it as well. Sadly, I don't think she's strong enough to fight it off like we did."

"I never knew of this." Commander Jay says.

"This must be their tactic to get the animals of Dungalo to go to war."

Meevo raises a brow. "War?"

And then Commander Jay tells them about the battle plan Prince Edgar and Princess Elena found.

"And so we need all the support we can get." Commander Jay concludes, looking at the faces of all the tigers.

The Tiger clan exchange looks that carried conversations that Commander Jay can't understand. However, their silent conversation is soon broken.

"The Tigers have always been known as solitary creatures that barely associate with other species," Mario begins. "This exile meant nothing to us, except for the shame of being cast out like criminals. We already planned to start our own exclusive community away from the rest of the animals."

Commander Jay deflates. "But—"

"However," Mario interrupts. "This has gone too far, posing us as criminals and taking some of our own. A tiger never forgets the injustice done to it. And so we have decided…"

"We will help," Meevo says,' flexing his right paw. Commander Jay shifts to

Raymond's side. "There is nothing I hate more than the feeling of shame, especially when I've done nothing to deserve it. Those vultures played us, and we fell right into their honey trap. Embarrassing."

"So, little critter." Raymond says, putting a light paw on Commander Jay. "What do you need us to do?"

Chapter Fourteen

"Everything is falling into place," Jerome says, fluffing his feathers as he perches on a table in the human commander's office. "In mere days, we'll launch an attack on the enemy Kingdom and take their lands. You get your crystals, and the Royalists keep their power.

The human male polishing his gun does not look up. He's silent for several seconds, and Jerome is beginning to wonder at all if he was heard when the human speaks, voice laced with condescension.

"Have I ever told you that you talk too much, vulture?" he says, raising his gun to the light to check for missed spots. "And with too much ego, it irks me. Because you speak like we can't get the crystals without the help of you critters."

Jerome's feathers twitch. "Without us, you would not even know where to look.

You'd still be drowning yourselves in swamps in search of crystals."

The human smirks, finally snapping the gun shut with a metallic click.

"Never make the mistake of taking us for fools or weaklings that can't take care of our matters," the human says. "You approached us and only quickened the process for us. But without you, we could've still found a way.

The human tuts.

"We already had our battle plans and strategy, but you willingly and selfishly made yourself a puppet," he says. "Yes, you were useful for a small part, but that does not give you the right to act like we're on equal footing."

"You needed us once," Jerome replies, voice tightening, "and you still do." The man rises slowly from his chair, gun held casually in hand.

"Since your little usefulness makes you feel important, let's give you that," the human says. "But we are probably the only beings that would ever need you. How pitiful is that?"

Jerome is quiet, holding back the words coming to him.

"You vultures are too drunk by an illusion of power, too corrupted by the evil that comes with power – greed," the human tsks. "It's pitiful, really, because the only time you ever feel something is—"

They hear a loud boom that rattles the walls and everything in the room, throwing them off balance and making the human release a startled stray shot at the ceiling.

The two of them are still as they both listen to the momentary silence. "What was that?" the human asks.

Jerome has no idea, but before he can even say anything, chaos ensues. Screams outside the base the humans have set up in Dungalo and rapid footsteps slapping against the floors in the hallways.

The human commander rushes to his window and flings it open. "What's happening!?"

The door to the human commander's office aggressively swings open, banging against the wall.

A human soldier stumbles in, face pale. "Sir, the Dungalo walls have been breached by some rebel animals! Led by their Prince!"

And yet another… "Sir, the collar tags are falling off the animals; they—" The commander whirls around in Jerome's direction, pointing his gun at him.

"You knew." His voice is low and dangerous.

"You dirty creature! This was your doing–"

Jerome bristles. "If the technology you invented failed, it's nothing to do with m —"

A gunshot explodes through the air, and Jerome squawks, hurling himself sideways as wood splinters across the table. Guards surge forward at the commander's bark.

"Seize him!"

Jerome flaps wildly, knocking over a lamp as he leaps to the rafters. Another shot whizzes past him and falters, crashing into the ceiling beams.

"Corner him!" the human commander snarls. "He does not leave alive!"

Jerome dives low to get to the window, but a guard lunges at him. He claws at him, slipping free and flying towards the open window.

There's another shot, and this time it hits him, brushing against his right wing in an explosion of dark feathers and blood. He screeches but manages to fly out the window in a barrage of gunshots that manage to miss him.

The commander lowers the smoking gun, chest rising with fury as he watches the vulture blend into the darkness of the night.

Another soldier rushes in, breathless. "Sir, the base for the hostage animals has been attacked! There's a female lion leading the attack, and the officers there can't fend them off."

The man's face twists into an ugly grimace.

"Deploy everything we have in Dungalo. Tanks, fire, all of it!" he nearly snarls like one of the animals. "We'll stick to *our* plan. Destroy everything and every animal in your path! We can't let go of the fortune when we just found it!"

The commander's order ripples out like a spark to dry grass. Outside, engines roar to life, and the humans invading Dungalo scramble into formation with their weapons raised. An alarm bell loudly shrieks through the night.

On the hill above the gates, the animals are already gathering.

Prince Edgar is in the front, and beside him is Princess Elena, fierce and strong.

They both catch each other's eyes and share a smile before looking back to the burning Kingdom.

."Together!" Princess Elena cries to both kingdoms. "If we fall, the land falls. If we stand, the land stands with us!"

An endless ocean of roars answers her; in addition to Dungalo citizens, her own Kingdom is racking in number, approved by her father, whom she made to understand that not only Dungalo was at stake if the humans take over.

In one cry, they charge — lions, tigers, bears, zebras, and little critters — and from the shadows, even the owls lift their voices.

The humans pour through the gates with their tanks and manpower, firing as they approach, but the animals are ready for this, protecting their formation with shields made from stone slabs and donated tortoise and turtle shells.

Then the animals move.

Porcupines roll forward first, firing spikes that drive the humans back behind their shields. Elephants follow closely behind, toppling the tanks and sending the humans back into the gates before they even have a chance to react.

Through the ranks, the tigers pull forward, sprinting in such speed and power that deters even the bravest-coloured

Mario leads, his dual-coloured stripes flashing in the glares of gunfire as he precisely barrels through a human line, clearing a path for the others to follow. Meevo leaps past him, claws flashing as he tackles a soldier straight into the mud.

"That's for my great grandpa!" he snarls before lashing at another human. "And that's for being accomplices in exiling us. Embarrassing, ugh!"

Raymond is at the rear, not as wild as his brothers but steady enough as he shields smaller animals and drives men back with sweeping blows.

"Stay close," he growls to a pair of hares before lunging forward to tear a rifle from a man's grasp.

"Dungalo holds!" Mario bellows, his roar cutting through the chaos.

From the sky, big birds dive, ripping shields and rifles from the human soldiers. The smaller, mischievous birds circle around the human's heads, causing confusion and great annoyance.

Suddenly, there's an explosion, and a voice cuts through. "They targeted the Glebel building!"

It seems the human strategy is to burn everything to the ground; more tanks are coming out, and Prince Edgar lunges on one, tearing open the metallic doors with his claws and scaring the human within. But there are still more.

"Elena!" he screams for the Princess and she gets the signal.

"Now!" she roars, and the sound is carried far, with other lions passing the message on.

From the shadows of her kingdom, reinforcements pour in. Stags with sharpened antlers, badgers with their teeth bared, and great bears rolling forward like boulders. Elena's people answer, their strength folding into the forces of Dungalo as one.

Together, they push against the humans.

There's another detonation near the Glebel that is targeted at the human base, but it sends the already weak walls of the Glebel folding in on themselves. When the smoke clears, only the debris of a great building remains.

However, with the reinforcements, the human ranks are starting to falter. More of their tanks are toppled by the elephants, their lines are being broken by huge animals barrelling into them, and their weapons are being snatched from them by the aerial offence.

"Fall back! Fall back!!!" the human commander screams, and it's even more encouragement for the animals to start driving them out of the fallen gates of Dungalo with zero mercy.

When silence finally creeps over the battlefield, Prince Edgar lifts his head and surveys the damage. There are certain parts of Dungalo on fire, but nothing the elephants can't take care of with their trunks splashing water from a spring.

Upturned tanks are everywhere, some still running and some still carrying unconscious humans, but they pose no threat because the head of the serpent has been cut off… or rather, has detached itself and run off on its own.

Princess Elena steps up beside Prince Edgar, her paw brushing his mane. He looks at her, then rubs his head against hers in a show of affection.

"We did it," he says, and she smiles. "We did it."

The meerkats climb the rubble of the Glebel, standing tall on their hind legs and scanning the horizon for any more danger.

When everything has been deemed safe, Commander Jay chirps sharply, releasing a signal and a message into the air.

The war is over, and Dungalo is theirs again.

Chapter Fifteen

*P*eace and joy reign once more in the city-state of Dungalo, and after nearly stepping into another dark era, this time, the animals know how to appreciate it more.

Glebel Hall has long been cleared of its debris, and the remaining structure knocked down. In the months following the Battle of Dungalo, Prince Edgar had proposed turning The Glebel into a central garden instead, to grow nature around the Neem tree that has stood strong and shielded them for centuries.

The Neem tree itself is fruiting, and on it are little monkeys hanging up colourful ribbons and lights and trinkets that make the majestic tree look even grander.

Below, animals are zapping back and forth from one location to another and constantly screaming out instructions or calls to help with some task.

It is an eventful day for the animals, indeed. In a couple of hours, an extremely symbolic event will be held at the base of the Neem tree. One that signifies unity and strength in togetherness.

It's the wedding ceremony between Prince Edgar and Princess Elena—an act that will solidify the merging of their two kingdoms as one.

Prince Edgar, mane groomed and crown gleaming, stands tall at the base of the Neem, looking at his soon-to-be queen walking down the aisle created by two rows of adoring animals.

Princess Elena is radiant as she walks elegantly, eyes fixed on the lion she had once thought impossible to get married to, but here they were now. Behind her are two rolls of the female section of the reinstated meerkat security force, whom she asked to be an honorary bridal train.

From the palace, Queen Sheila watches from her chamber's balcony in silence. Her mind has been stretched beyond its limits, and she still is in the process of recovery, her eyes soften with pride. Though she cannot rule anymore, she has lived long enough to see her son crowned and her kingdom mended. That is enough.

Behind her are several maids and two

physicians at her call, in case she goes into another episode that came with her recovery. One where she loses all thoughts and starts acting on autopilot, being prone to danger.

The physicians don't know if she will fully heal, but they do their best to keep her away from triggers—crowds, noise, and even silence. A calm state of mind is recommended for her, as it was recommended for her late husband.

So there are constantly harpists in her room, usually taking shifts to play calming music and strike that balance between noise and silence.

Although Queen Sheila can't possibly see herself falling into an episode today. She is far too happy for her son on this day to let herself sleep.

The Cheetahs might be the only ones in a bit of a gloom, pouting at the back of the crowds for having had their short-lived title stripped from them. However, they can't complain much because they were let go without serious punishment.

They were said to be under the dark magic of the vultures because their constant greed led them to listen to the polished words of the Royalists' offer to get them into a position of power. So even if they might have wanted that position, they can't be prosecuted for acting under the royalists' spell.

The Royalists, however, are the ones who got the worst of it all for all their century-long wickedness. We won't speak much about them, but just know that they were banished forever from the merged city-state of Dungalo, bound forever to the empty sky and condemned to wander without a home. Their shadows stretch thin across the ground, yet no animal looks up.

And at the edges of the crowd, the meerkats take their post. Confident, they stand on their hind legs, scanning the horizon. They do not relax, even on a day of peace. For their eyes are the first to see, and their voice is the first to call a warning.

From this day, it is no longer a question of proving their worth. It is the way of their people.

And so it is told: meerkats stand on their hind legs to keep watch, for the kingdom, for each other, and for the peace they fought to win.

www.ingramcontent.com/pod-product-compliance
Lightning Source LLC
Chambersburg PA
CBHW07081925062
47170CB00006B/2164